D1100854

The Egyptian Codex

David Ian Flynn

11th
STOREY
PRESS

For my Mee Lee

The Egyptian Codex
Copyright © 2019 David Ian Flynn.
Published by Eleventh Storey Press, Singapore.

All rights reserved. No part of this publication may be reproduced, distributed, or transmitted in any form or by any means, including photocopying, recording, or other electronic or mechanical methods, without the prior written permission of the copyright owner.

This is a work of fiction. Names, characters, businesses, places, events and incidents are either the products of the author's imagination or used in a fictitious manner. Any resemblance to actual persons, living or dead, or actual events is purely coincidental.

ISBN: 978-981-14-3413-6 (paperback)

ISBN: 978-981-14-3169-2 (e-book)

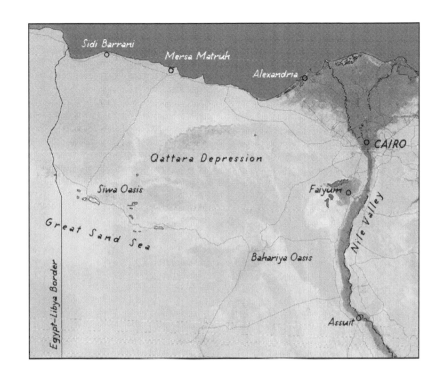

Map of Northern Egypt

Prologue

Siwa, Egypt, 1942

For a day and a night, it rained in the oasis. Brick walls turned to mud, and the streets ran red with the slurry. The older residents had called it a bad omen. However, to one farmer named Isri, it seemed like good fortune. Where the water had been channelled down across his property, an earth-bank had collapsed. Amongst the rubble, he found sealed earthenware pots, their necks just protruding from the mud. Prising the stopper off one, he discovered they were full of parchments — brown like dried leaves and covered in black ink scratchings.

By a stroke of luck, Isri knew what they were. Foreigners had been digging up such fragments close to his cousin's village near Faiyum, south of Cairo, for several years. He guessed they would pay handsomely for such a rare and substantial find. It was a month-long camel journey through Bahariya to the Nile. A time consuming and not inexpensive journey, though less arduous than the trip northward and along the coast, through the many military checkpoints — but maybe worth the outlay, he thought. He removed a piece of papyrus to confirm his discovery and then recovered the pots, packing down the soil and placing several palm fronds over the area. The following day, Isri left with only a brief mention to his neighbour that he was off to visit his cousin.

Several weeks later, the arrival of a foreigner from Mersa Matruh was of little interest to Isri's neighbour. This stranger had stayed up at the small two-storey hotel on the spur of the Gebel al-Mantra. However, the next day, the foreigner paid him a visit, bringing the hotel owner with him to translate his questions into the Berber tongue of the oasis. The foreigner was dressed in a white suit and spoke a language the hotel owner had said was Italian.

Apparently, Isri had died of malaria, but before passing had revealed to the stranger that some old documents had been discovered on his land. The neighbour told him he couldn't recall Isri mentioning anything of this. Finally, the foreigner asked if he could show him the farmer's land. For two days, the Italian sketched and measured the place, then as quickly as he had come, he left.

Chapter 1

Oxford, England, present day

Oxford had been Michael's life — its limestone walls filled his memories. The streets he cycled down now were as familiar to him as ... well, anything he could remember. Slipping past the elaborate gate of All Souls, he turned down a side alley and crossed over a courtyard. It was early morning and there was almost no one around. Michael stopped outside a wooden building that seemed to sprout from one of the ancient walls. This had been his world for the past two years — actually since graduating.

His hand turned the door-knob and pushed the door open. The exotic smell of oudh pervaded the air. Burning this incense had been Frank's habit since he had returned from the markets of Khan el-Kalili in Cairo the year before. Frank was more than just Michael's fellow worker. He had been a good friend of his father and they had much in common.

As usual for this time of the day, Frank was standing next to the kettle, whistling while waiting for it to boil. His wild grey eyebrows arched up in query as he held up a teapot. Michael nodded and walked through to the office and his desk — an old wooden pedestal desk. This he had liberated from an empty room in one of the College's hallowed wings. Frank had helped him carry it out last winter when the heating had broken down and the building abandoned for the day. They had almost been caught when a porter had appeared from nowhere and they'd been forced to hide beneath it until he had gone.

The hut was an extension of the Ancient Document Registry. It contained much of the College's collection of uncatalogued parchment and papyrus documents. There were several storage rooms with humidity and temperature control, to keep the environment pretty much constant. The rooms were filled with shelves and on these were wooden trays which contained the actual fragments. Generally, the trays contained materials that were obtained at the same time, although these could actually date from several periods. There were specimens of not only papyrus but cloth and paper, with writing in almost every early Near Eastern script: Aramaic, Egyptian Hieroglyphics, Hieratic, Demotic,

Coptic, Hebrew, Greek, Latin, Syrian, Parthian and Persian.

Michael's work involved the conservation and identification of these materials. Each day, he would begin with inspecting the specimen for any damage, removing any loose debris and dirt, and fixing any errant pieces. He would then record the type and content of the document in a catalogue: its language, origin and a brief description of the text and of the condition of each piece. Next, he took a photograph of the artifact, front and back, and listed all of the information online. Researchers and academics in the appropriate field could then elect to translate the text. To help Michael identify the language, there were examples of all the relevant types posted on the walls. However, he rarely needed to look at them. Understanding languages came almost without effort — a skill he had seemingly inherited from his grandfather.

After detailing all this information, the specimen was carefully sandwiched between special polyester sheets and a temporary seal applied around the edges. This system had replaced the more traditional method of placing it between two sheets of glass and taping the sides a few years before. If the piece was discovered to be of some significance, it was then transferred to the main University Archives for more permanent preservation.

The collection had been acquired from mostly two sources: donations from wealthy travellers and dealers, and those acquired by university staff during archaeological expeditions. Most fragments and manuscripts had some preliminary paperwork — details of how they were obtained with some notes on their history, though by no means all.

As Michael sat down, he reached for the catalogue and perused the previous day's entry. It had been a good day: a late period hieratic text, a part of a Greek literary work and a Roman land record. However, today was slightly unusual. They had come to the end of the classification of manuscripts in Store Room 1 the day before. Now, they started on Store Room 2. It was with some ceremony that Frank took out the key to the room, unlocked the door and switched on the lights. One by one, fluorescent tubes flickered on, revealing row after row of shelves. Michael could swear it was twice the size of the previous storeroom. Four more years of work, he thought resignedly.

He picked up a tray from a nearby shelf and with a nod to Frank, who was checking the climate controls, took it to his desk. Inside was a large brown envelope, sealed with wax. This was unusual but not unheard of. Breaking the seal, he slid the contents onto his desk. In front of him lay a folded sheet of paper and a fairly ordinary cream envelope, on which a badly scrawled address had been hand-written. There was a stamp in the top right-hand corner — faint black printing covered the face of a young man wearing a fez, a type of hat worn by men in the Middle-East. Michael put it down, unfolded the single piece of paper and read its contents.

To Whom It May Concern,

Inside this envelope is a scrap of some old document. It belonged to my father, who recently passed away. I do not think it has any historical significance but I do not know what to do with it, so please accept it as a donation to the college.

It was dated two years before and signed off by a Mr John Atherton with an address somewhere in Oxfordshire.

Michael turned the cream envelope over and lifted the flap. At one time it had been sealed, but the glue had dried, leaving a brown residue on both surfaces. Inside was the actual fragment. It was about three inches by four and made of papyrus, with the mottled colouring of dried tobacco leaves. Three of the edges were badly flaking and there were two holes near one side. Dark brown writing covered the complete piece. Evidently, it must have come from a much larger document.

He opened his desk drawer and took out a magnifying glass. Peering through it, he started a detailed examination of the writing on the front. The writing direction was from left to right. There was no punctuation and no spaces between the words. Its language was superficially Coptic, though written not in the more usual uncials, or capitalised form, but in a scrawled cursive hand. Coptic was a form of writing that had begun in Egypt in the first century AD. However, even with his gift for languages, Michael struggled to understand what the document was about. Many of the characters were unusual and curiously formed. As he scanned the text for meaning, something stopped him in his tracks. Never had he seen anything like this before. Right at the bottom of the text was a different language — Aramaic.

The incongruity of it completely stunned him. He sat staring at it for a while and then he began to translate it. Immediately Michael realised it included a name. *Shim'on* followed by the word *qan'ana'*. What was an obviously Jewish name doing in an Egyptian document, he thought? Michael called out, 'Frank. Have you got a moment?' Frank unfolded himself from his chair and walked over.

'What is it, lad?' He stooped down, put his hand on Michael's shoulder and peered at the fragment. Michael's finger pointed at the Aramaic name.

'Hmm,' Frank murmured.

'What do you make of it?' Michael enquired.

Frank slowly translated it under his breath. 'Shimon. Simon Kan'anai.' He stood up, stretched his back and looked up at the ceiling. 'Simon,' he repeated.

'Who was that?'

'There's only one historical person I know with that title. He was also known as Simon Zealotes. Simon the Canaanite. Tenth disciple of Jesus.'

Chapter 2

Upper Egypt, present day

The thin man in a stained linen suit slid from the donkey. He pulled a white cloth from his pocket and wiped his face. The green verdant ribbon of the Nile valley was a half day journey behind and an arduous trek up through sun-scorched escarpments. In front of him was the white-washed building that the French priest had told him about. A single crucifix adorned the arch of its doorway.

He briefly wondered if finally, this might be the place he was looking for. It had taken him three years of patient searching to bring him to this point. Hidden somewhere within these walls, he hoped he would find the secret sayings of God.

Akhmim was the most likely place, the thin man had theorised. It stood on the right bank of the river Nile, seventy miles south of the Upper Egyptian town of Assiut. The hills surrounding it were filled with monasteries, some dating back thousands of years. Why they were drawn to this area, in such numbers, no one knew. But it could be its ancient connection with Asmodeus, king of all demons. Here, it was said, the angel Raphael had fought and then imprisoned the demon — the very creature that had built the great Temple of Jerusalem. It was an unearthly place where God and the world of man had collided. What better place than this to store the secrets of heaven?

Chapter 3

Oxford, England, present day

'What do you make of it?' Michael finally asked
Frank. 'Most of the text looks like a sort of
cursive Coptic.'

'Which excavation did it come from?'

Michael knew Frank was referring to the
archaeological site where it was found. They
were always much more wary of artifacts that
had been purchased directly from dealers. Often
the provenances of such pieces were clouded by
half-truths and lies.

'No site. It was … just in this.' Michael held up
the beige envelope. 'No other information
included.'

'Mmm. I can't say that I've seen anything like
this before,' Frank replied. Scrutinizing the
fragment of papyrus over his glasses, he turned
the piece over. On the reverse, Michael could see
a handful of characters, all of them Demotic —
an even earlier Egyptian writing system that had
its beginnings around 400BC. Finally Frank
remarked, 'Three different scripts from three
different eras. A biblical figure, a writing system

typically used to record Egyptian magical spells, and glyphs that aren't even used correctly.' He thought for a moment. 'Mmm. A patchwork of phrases lifted from disparate texts and mechanically copied out. At best, it's from a scribe practising different scripts. At worst, it's a hoax.'

Frank put his hand on Michael's shoulder. 'There is no end of fakes and forgeries — both now and in the distant past. Where there are people to be fooled or money to be made...' He saw the disappointment on Michael's face. 'Look, don't waste your time on it. Put it in the scrap pile. The undergraduate students can use it for restoration practice.'

Michael knew Frank was probably right. Even the most erudite of people had been outwitted by clever forgeries. The one that came to mind was that of the Vinland map. In 1957, a map and accompanying text had been discovered in Spain. The map purported to be an original fifteenth century Norse depiction of the world. What was so significant was its illustration of a new landmass where North America lay. It even stated that this land was first visited in the eleventh century, well before the time of Columbus. It was offered to Yale University, who subjected it to expert scrutiny over several years before declaring it authentic. However, over the following years, more and more questions arose over certain features. The map showed the northern tip of Greenland, which had only been discovered in the twentieth century. And handwriting analysis indicated a relatively modern hand must have composed the inscriptions.

Frank held out the wooden tray they generally kept for all the dubious or worthless items and gave it a little shake. With a shrug, Michael popped the artifact in. Frank frowned, 'You know that the very first Christian manuscripts were written in Greek.'

'But …,' Michael started.

'Yes, I know there's some controversy that the documents were translated from an unknown Hebrew or Aramaic version,' interrupted Frank. 'But until there is more evidence … the best conclusion is that they were originally written in Greek. Let's not even think about Egyptian.'

Although Palestine at the time of Jesus was a multi-lingual society, only Aramaic, Hebrew, Greek and a little Latin were spoken. Even so, as the morning wore on, the mysterious nature of the document grew on Michael, and when Frank went for lunch, he went to the tray, slipped the papyrus back into its original envelope and placed it in the top drawer of his desk.

Picking up the folded sheet of paper from Mr John Atherton, he put that into his bag. Michael thought he would check that out later as well. The remainder of the afternoon passed slowly as he catalogued a Ptolemaic marriage licence and he was pretty tired when he finally said farewell to Frank and cycled home.

Locking his bicycle to the railings outside his place, Michael walked up the stone steps and let himself in. He immediately felt a sense of peace and order. The small terraced house had been bought by his grandfather, which in turn had been left to Michael's own father. Both of them had been academics — Michael's grandfather, an expert in Semitic languages and his father, an archaeologist specialising in Persian antiquities. Each had been driven to uncover the mysteries of the past, often at the expense of everything else. Michael rarely saw either of them as he was growing up. In fact, the last thing his father had done was to get him the position at the Registry. That was just before he took off to the Middle-East and his untimely heart attack.

The house was still eerily reminiscent of him, though. Framed maps and drawings lined the walls of the study and living room; layouts of archaeological sites annotated with red chinagraph pencil and sketches of tombs and temples throughout Mesopotamia. Michael ran his hand along the bureau and picked up his father's traditional brass theodolite. He swore it seemed to get heavier each time he did this.

Michael went to one of the bookshelves and pulled down a thick telephone directory with curled pages. Collapsing onto the living room sofa, he also withdrew the letter from Mr Atherton, contemplated the note for a while and then picked up the directory. Flicking through to the front, he searched out the name. There were several Athertons, but only one with the initial J who was living in Oxfordshire.

Michael lifted the telephone and dialled the number. It rang five times, then was answered by a man with a clipped accent. 'Hello. Atherton here. Who's this?'

'Hello Mr Atherton. My name is Michael from the Ancient Document Registry. I was calling about something you donated to the University a few years back.'

There was a brief silence before the voice returned, 'Blimey. I'd forgotten all about that. Look, I'm in a bit of a hurry. I have to go out. Can you call tomorrow?'

'Sure …,' Michael started to say. Then, on the spur of the moment, asked, 'Would it be all right if I come and talk to you in person?'

'Tomorrow?'

Michael confirmed this, and after a brief hesitation, Mr Atherton agreed. 'I live in Kirtlington. Hope Farm. Can you make it before noon?'

Michael replied he could and the man on the other end of the line then proceeded to give him directions.

The following morning was clear and sunny. Before leaving for the railway station, Michael called the Registry. Frank answered and was a little concerned that Michael wasn't coming in. Michael wasn't sure why he made up a story of coming down with flu-like symptoms, but he was a bit uneasy about explaining his interest in the document. Especially as Frank had so emphatically concluded the fragment was a fake — that and the fact that Michael had taken it without permission.

Kirtlington was a small village north of Oxford and easily reachable from the nearby station at Tackley. Michael took his bike on the train and cycled the three miles, across the River Cherwell, to Hope Farm. It was a half timber, half stone-built house, surrounded by a small copse of silver birch trees. John Atherton answered the door soon after the first knock. He was a large man in his early fifties. His fair hair was thinning, and he had a firm handshake. 'So what can I do for you?' he said as soon as they were seated at the kitchen table.

Michael introduced himself and explained the work they did at the Registry. And how the sheer volume of documents meant that there was a backlog in their categorisation. And if Mr Atherton could provide any more information on the piece, he had donated to the College, it would help in narrowing down its origin.

John Atherton nodded towards the back of the kitchen. On a bookshelf was a black and white photograph portraying a smiling lad, wearing khaki shorts and shirt, leaning against a palm tree. 'Well, there's not much to tell, really. I found it in my dad's old army things. When he passed away five years ago, I put all his stuff in the spare room. Then two years back, I decided to sort it out. I came across that envelope with the old thing in it and couldn't make head nor tail of it. So I sent it to the Dean at my old college and forgot all about it.'

'What did your father do in the war?' Michael asked him.

'He was mostly in North Africa. You know, fighting the Desert Fox.'

'Right,' Michael said hesitantly.

'He was called up in 1942. Then he got posted out to Tunisia as part of Operation Torch.'

'What was that?' Michael asked.

'What do they teach at school nowadays?' Mr Atherton sounded slightly irked.

The old soldier's son then spent the next ten minutes giving Michael a short history of the North African Campaign.

It had started with the Italian leader, Mussolini, seeking to expand his North African territory at the beginning of the war. The Italians had for many years controlled Libya and so they moved eastward towards Egypt, which was then only lightly guarded by the British. They made a swift advance and reached Sidi Barrani, fifty miles inside the Egyptian border before digging in and fortifying defensive positions. But then the British counter-attacked and pushed the Italians back into Libya. Hitler, worried that he was about to lose the entire Mediterranean, ordered a new German army, the Afrika Korps, under Erwin Rommel to hold the line. Rommel, nicknamed the Desert Fox, not only did that, but he eventually forced the British all the way back to Mersa Matruh, deep inside Egypt. They also took the oasis at Siwa. But he was poorly resupplied, running out of fuel and replacement tanks. With only a slim chance to strike for the Nile, he had no option but to hold up. The British had time to reinforce and attacked at El Alamein, eventually causing the Italian and German armies to retreat. Soon afterwards, the Allies landed troops all along the coast of Algeria and Morocco as part of the Torch invasions. The Allied armies kept pushing the Germans back and finally forced their surrender in Tunisia in May 1943.

'So he was never in Egypt?' Michael said quizzically.

'No. The Eight Army was in 1941, but my dad joined up too late for that. He was always based in Tunisia with the 78th Infantry Division. He saw a lot of fighting as Rommel fought to cover his retreat. But the Germans and Italians finally surrendered in '43. One of my dad's favourite stories was how he had to guard endless lines of prisoners all by himself.'

'Well, at least he came back.'

'Yeah. But he was invalided out. He got some shrapnel from a land-mine later that year. They brought him home in a hospital ship. '

'So you have no idea where he got that papyrus from?'

'No. He never said anything about it. I only found it amongst his stuff after he died.'

Chapter 4

Oxford, England, present day

The public house was an old Victorian building adjoining a lock on the River Thames. Solidly built from limestone, it sat on the riverbank with an air of quiet permanence. Upstream was Christchurch meadow and the stretch of the river prized by the university rowers. Far in the distance, across the green flood-fields, rose the cathedral spire and ornate college roofs.

Michael sat outside with a pint of local pale ale and let the late afternoon sun warm him, still thinking about what he ought to do next. He flicked open the catch on his bag and took out the folder in which he had carefully secured the papyrus and envelope. This he unfastened and examined the document. There were ten lines of text, each with about twenty characters, all written continuously together. Michael retrieved his notebook and copied out some of the lines. Above certain characters, he made his best guess at what they represented, but he just didn't have the expertise to figure it out completely.

With a sigh, Michael put everything back into his bag and closed it up. Just as he leant back and reached out for his drink, he was jolted by a young woman who was trying to squeeze pass the table. His glass toppled to the floor and smashed in a shower of foam.

'Whoa! Wasn't looking where I was going,' the girl cried out before Michael had time to react. Behind her were a group of young adults in very high spirits. The girl, dark tousled-haired, wearing a combat jacket and jeans, lingered a few feet away. She turned to her friends and called, 'You go on ahead. I'll buy this … lad another drink.' The others waved cheerfully to her and set off up the towpath.

The girl looked at him expectantly, her head tipped to one side.

'Will you join me?' Michael's question even surprised him. She hesitated briefly, and then nodded before disappearing inside to the bar, returning with two drinks after a while. A young member of the bar staff followed her out with a pan and brush and swiftly cleaned the area.

'What are you celebrating?' Michael enquired after the youth had left.

'My first publication in Oxford.' She smiled hesitantly. 'Well, my name is on the paper.'

'I'm impressed.'

'Don't be. It's not that brilliant. I am at the end of a long list. But, hey, I'm on it.'

'What's it about?'

'The non-periodicity of radioactive decay.'

Michael's face must have shown how little of this he grasped. She laughed and continued, 'Several years ago, research started to suggest that there was a periodic fluctuation in radioactive decay.'

'No. Still a bit lost,' Michael admitted sheepishly.

'Okay, you know how all atoms are made up of a nucleus and surrounding electrons.'

Michael nodded his head to show that he was following her now. It was some time since he had studied science, but he knew the basics.

'Well, in some atoms, the nucleus every so often ejects a particle, quite unpredictably. This is radioactive decay. Totally random.' She spoke with enviable ease. 'However, researchers in Germany, and a few other places, started to analyse the number of particles being ejected and found that it peaked at certain times of the year. This was quite a shock. Some scientist theorised it could be due to the annual variation in the Earth-Sun distance, others suggested changes in the number of solar neutrinos. If true, it would have had a major impact on our understanding of what was going on inside the atom. Well, we designed new detectors, repeated the experiments and found no deviation.'

'You mean, you got published proving something … didn't happen?' asked Michael, incredulously.

'Yeah. How great is that! But that's what science is all about. Observing, theorising, testing and if the theory is wrong, debunking.'

'So that's what you do? Nuclear Physics.'

'Correct. But I am just about finished here.'

'What do you mean?'

'I'm on a post-doctoral sabbatical. My time in Oxford is almost up. My main place of work is in Tucson. University of Arizona.'

'You're American?'

'Yep. But don't hold it against me.' The girl laughed. 'No accent, right?'

'No.'

'My parents moved to England when I was ten. They only moved back to the States a few years ago.'

'Nice to meet you ...?' Michael said, putting out his hand.

'Anna,' she replied, shaking it and giving him a playful smile.

'Anna from Arizona. I am Michael. From Oxford.'

Chapter 5

Oxford, England, present day

The sun set and they moved inside. The long summer evenings were coming to an end and there was a distinct chill to the air.

'What is it that you do?' she asked once they had bought another round and found seats in a quiet corner.

'Papyrology is its official name. Preserve and catalogue old documents essentially.' She looked at him expectedly, as if he had more to say. 'It was my grandfather's passion, really. He taught himself Greek and Coptic and joined the University in the 1930s. He worked on the vast haul of texts that were discovered at Bahnasa.'

El-Bahnasa was a town that lay west of the Nile and a good way south of Cairo. Per-Medjed, the ancient Egyptians called it. For thousands of years it thrived. Some say it became the third largest city in the whole of the country. But its fortune waned and the canal it was built beside fell into disrepair. It was eventually abandoned and for a thousand years the sand slowly covered it. But the city was to be reborn as the population grew and new land was required. The canal was dug out and roads built. Finally, after another thousand years, it became famous again. The city's ancient rubbish mounds yielded a flood of fragments, variously inscribed with horoscopes, tax assessments, wills, plays, poems, and letters — in fact, every kind of ancient document.

'It's what he loved. That sense of the unknown. The ancient text that he held in his hands might be nothing more than a mundane receipt ... but it could also be a Greek epic, never heard or seen before.'

'What about you?' she questioned.

'I just drifted into it. It was related to what my father had done too. It just seemed like the easiest thing to do.'

'That is just so ... off the chart. I thought what I did was super academic, but what you do is ... scholarly.'

Self-consciously, Michael straightened up and tried to appear less studious. It obviously didn't work as she only just stifled a burst of laughter.

For several minutes, they sat in companionable silence. Michael was mesmerised by the girl. Her china blue eyes never straying far from his. She was alarmingly direct, yet there was something almost childlike in her innocence.

'Do you carbon date any of your documents?' she enquired finally.

Carbon dating was the standard test to determine the age of organic remains. It was pretty reliable out to 50,000 years.

'No. Not really. There is a centre over in the Institute of Archaeology, but Frank rarely sends anything there. We don't have the budget to do much.'

'Frank?'

'He runs the Registry where I work.'

'Then how do you figure out when something was written?'

'Well, over time, writing in any language, changes. The style, letter formation, use of particular words all evolve over the years. Sometimes you get lucky and a known event or person is mentioned. From that, you can pinpoint a range of dates for that type of writing. Anything similar to it could, in all likelihood, be dated to the same period. I mean it's not very precise but a specialist can usually narrow down the date to within fifty to a hundred years or so.'

'So about the same as carbon dating,' Anna mused.

'Do you know something of that? Carbon dating, I mean,' Michael remarked.

'Yeah. I've done my fair share of it in the past. My supervisor was involved with some of the analysis of the Qumran Cave scrolls. So as a grad student I did a lot of work off the back of that for him.'

Now this was something Michael was familiar with. He knew all about the Qumran caves. The discovery in 1946 of scrolls and papyrus fragments in the Judean desert was a major archaeological event. Eventually nearly a thousand texts were unearthed over the following decade. More usually called the Dead Sea Scrolls, their origin was thought to be from a sect called the Essenes but also could be a cache of documents from libraries in Jerusalem, buried shortly after the Romans destroyed the Temple there in 70AD.

'That must have been exciting?' Michael stated.

'Yes, and no. The scrolls were tested twenty years ago. But it made the Lab more established, so it got ever more requests to accurately date other archaeological finds. In general, it means lots of late nights. Lots of sample preparation and equipment calibration.'

Michael pulled the folder out of his bag and showed the fragment to Anna. 'This is the thing that is intriguing me now.'

She looked it over but after a moment just shook her head. 'Looks like gibberish.'

'Yes, I guess it does. But no more than calculus does to me.'

Later, they wandered back towards town, cutting across the river meadow. The sky was a deep mauve masked by several clouds which glowed with an eerie light so that only the brightest stars appeared. One star in particular, low down in the south, shone out with a noticeable ice-blue intensity.

'That's Rigel,' Anna said, following Michael's gaze. 'A supergiant, hundreds of times larger than our own sun.'

Michael stared at her blankly. He didn't know any constellations other than Orion and the Big Dipper. And he certainly didn't know the names of any stars.

'We owe everything to stars like that.'

'What do you mean?' Michael asked.

'What we are today are the remnants from events, which occurred millions of years ago and billions of miles away. Your body has atoms from the simplest hydrogen to heavy ones, like calcium and iron. The simplest could have come from the moment the universe was created. But the heavier ones come from the expanding shock waves of exploding super suns. Rigel is such a super sun. They burn hot and fast, consuming their hydrogen fuel in a few million years. Then they swell, becoming bloated and red. Finally, they detonate. Unimaginable heat and pressure, forcing atoms to smash together. Sequentially becoming larger and larger. The core shrinks in seconds to become a super dense dwarf. The outer shell blasted into space, carrying with it all those life-essential elements.'

Michael stopped walking and tried to take in what she had just said. 'Star ash. Is that what you are saying we're made from?' he finally responded.

'Yep.' Then she paused, closed her eyes and recited, "The last long lap is the hardest, and I shall be dumped where the weed decays, and the rest is rust and stardust".'

'Poetry? Yours?'

'Vladimir Nabokov's words. Not mine.'

Michael and Anna walked in silence for a long while. His heart was heavy as he pondered the realisation that he was not, as he had so naively assumed, made from some shiny new molecules — each brought into existence for his own personal benefit by the powerful force of life. He was the recycled atoms of tens, maybe even hundreds, of wrecked stars, all long dead a life age ago. Mind you, he thought, it was somehow fitting that they were not the superior quality product they thought they were, but the detritus of an adolescent universe.

'Cheer up,' she cried, poking him with her finger.

Then she danced ahead, her scarf streaming behind her, slowing after a while to allow him to catch up. They strolled together like this, Anna doing the talking for the most part, for many hours. Cobbled streets rang with their footsteps. The city was asleep, the colleges dormant. Michael followed her across bridges and through arches until they came to a narrow doorway, steps hidden in shadow. He got the impression that she had been aiming for this place all along.

She took his hand and led him up the stairs — pulling him behind, silent and purposeful. The stairway seemed to go on and on, but eventually it opened out onto a small space, partly enclosed by a limestone wall with an opening set within it. Its gate had a broken lock and she unhooked the piece of wire that held it shut. They walked out onto the roof. Before them was the immense expanse of sky — grey, thread through with strands of vermillion. Dawn had finally arrived. The timing was impressive.

Rain began to slowly fall. Drops slid through the air and connected with Anna's upturned face. Her mouth parted and she licked her lips. Her hands went to her face and she gestured to her tongue. Tentatively, Michael ran his tongue over his top lip. The rain was slightly salty.

'I think the sky is crying,' she remarked.

Chapter 6

Oxford, England, present day

Michael looked up at the number above the entrance to the shop house. It was the same as the one Anna had given him. She had texted him earlier in the day asking if he wanted to meet up for lunch. The address was on the other side of Jericho near the wharves on Oxford Canal, so he had cycled over. Pushing open the door, Michael entered a dark and cluttered space. There was a strong smell of chemicals and the hum of some equipment he didn't quite recognize.

Anna was lying prone across a black couch. Her shirt was off and she was stripped down to a black bra, unhooked — the ends hanging down either side of her. Her back was exposed and he could see the bumps of vertebrae running down her spine. Crouching over her was a large Asian man who was focusing on something he was drawing on her smooth skin. She tilted her head towards Michael. 'Come, sit next to me.' He sidled over and squeezed himself into a small space between the couch and wall. 'This is Jung Gi,' she gestured with a slight movement of her head. The man grunted but didn't stop working.

Michael still hadn't uttered a word but watched in fascination as her skin was repeatedly pricked by the man. Michael's heart thumped in his chest and he felt his face begin to flush. Anna laughed, 'You look like you haven't seen a girl's back before.'

'No.' His voice was a little squeaky. He tried to lower it a bit, 'I mean yes. Many times.'

'Many times,' she repeated. 'That sounds like you're bragging.'

'No. You know, on the beach. Swimming pool,' Michael said, flustered.

He realised the man was tattooing a very intricate spiral-like design. In fact, he was almost finished. As he worked, the man used a black-stained cloth to wipe away excess ink. Then he tapped Anna on her shoulder, pushed back from the couch and proceeded to tidy up his tools.

'When did you decide … you know … to get a tattoo?' Michael asked.

Anna slid off the couch and faced him. He tried not to stare at her semi-naked body. Then she fastened her bra, pulled on her shirt and started to do up the buttons. 'Months back. Most of the work was done a while ago. Today was just some finer detail. Not so painful, thank goodness.' Anna pulled on a black leather jacket. 'Why don't you get inked?' she enquired.

'No. I hadn't thought of it.'

'Never?'

'No.' Michael really hadn't. Not for himself. But it was something on which his father had made a name for himself. He had been part of an archaeological team that had discovered an ancient burial site that contained the mummified corpse of a woman. When the wrappings were removed, she was remarkably well-preserved and found to be covered in tattoos with a geometric sequence of dots and dashes. The prevailing thought had been that she was a dancing girl or even a prostitute. But Michael's father had argued that she was a high priestess — the tattoos forming a kind of whole body amulet; a magical charm for protection.

'You should think about it. Jung Gi is unsurpassed. He comes from Korea and is only in town for a few months. This isn't his usual gig though. He's normally a full-time book illustrator.'

'What's the design?' Michael asked, sidestepping the issue.

'There is an idea that the universe is at heart, harmonious and symmetrical — that every particle has another complimentary cousin. This is Jung Gi's interpretation of that theory.'

Michael didn't know what to say, so he just nodded.

'Come on, let's get something to eat. I'm starving.' She gave the Korean a tight hug and thanked him.

'I've been following him for years. He has an incredible talent. Very edgy. When I heard he was here in Oxford, I had to get him to do a tattoo for me.' As she chatted on about the artist, Michael quietly pushed his bicycle alongside her. They ate in a small vegetarian café not far away, sitting on metal stools and eating off recycled paper plates.

Michael was wiping his mouth with a napkin when he caught a glimpse of his watch. 'I'm going to have to get back to work.' He was already ten minutes late, so he made his way outside.

'Great. You can give me a lift back,' Anna stated.

'On my bike?'

'Yes. You dope.'

Michael hesitated, but she had already sat sideways on the rack at the back of his bicycle.

'Where do you want me to drop you?'

'It's okay, go back to work and I'll walk from there. I've got some things to do in town.'

The ride back was a bit erratic as he tried to adjust to the unfamiliar weight, but having Anna wrap her arms around his waist more than made up for it. They reached the Registry after a while and Anna slid off the back of the bike.

Michael was about to ask her if she wanted to go out the next day when Frank stepped out of the main door. Michael thought he must have been watching out of the window. Frank looked unusually peevish. With an outstretched hand, Michael introduced the girl. 'Frank, this is Anna. She's a nuclear physicist.'

Frank coughed and nodded an acknowledgement. 'Scientist. Right.'

Michael had temporarily forgotten that Frank was really old school — very conservative and a believer in the literal truth. Anna stepped forward and shook Frank's hand. 'Michael has told me something of what you do here. It must be painstaking work.'

'It has its moments of excitement. The Registry was the first to identify a palimpsest of Galatians.'

Anna raised her eyebrows and gave a little shake of her head. 'Galatians?' she asked tentatively.

'The earliest copy of a book from the New Testament,' Frank added.

'Ah. Religion.'

'We are not theologians, although I do have a Masters in Religious Philosophy. We are more … explorers … discoverers.' Frank seemed pleased with his explanation.

'I thought us scientists were the explorers.'

'Not as far as the truth is concerned,' he admonished. Anna's eyebrows arched in obvious disagreement. Oblivious to this, Frank carried on, 'Unfortunately, science reduces everything to equations and models. It disregards the human existence. Nothing can be known absolutely. Reality is essentially unknowable.'

'But Religion is the complete anathema of science. It isn't based on observation, reflection and proof. It relies on revelation only.'

Frank eyed her suspiciously. 'But people don't believe in science. They don't trust experts anymore.'

Anna bristled at this. 'The universe is way too complex. This uncertainty is always going to exist. Our understanding of the world will always be in flux as we search for better ways of explaining reality. And humans can't stand ambiguity. They will always make their own interpretations.'

Frank shook his head. 'Scientists have brought that upon themselves. I think they make too many assertions. They are too certain. For every expert that claims one thing, you can find another who states the opposite.'

'Frankly, I don't agree.' Anna stopped, putting her hand over her mouth.

Frank smiled weakly, 'Hmm.'

Michael decided to intervene. 'Maybe you'll have to agree to disagree on this one.'

Anna shrugged and smiled, 'Sure.'

Frank retreated back towards the door. 'I'll see you in a bit, Michael.' Then he disappeared inside.

'Phew. That was a bit awkward,' Anna said.

'Don't mind Frank. He is passionate about the old ways. He distrusts anything new.'

'I'd hardly call science new.'

'Oh well, you know what I mean. Look, I have to get back to work. Frank is going off to a departmental meeting later, and I thought I'd take the opportunity to study some of the reference texts. I need to decode the papyrus I showed you.'

'Why are you so struck on that particular fragment?'

'Do you realise what it could mean? There are many copies of handwritten Christian texts. All are copies of copies. To find a document that was written by an original author … it would be sensational. A hundred years ago only a handful of papyri were known. Even now, we know of only a hundred that survived from the earliest centuries.'

'What does it say?'

'Look, I am no scholar. The Registry acts as a kind of …' Michael struggled to think of an appropriate analogy. 'Like a triage station. It's the first instance that many of these ancient documents are appraised. The actual translation and precise dating is the responsibility of others who have far more experience than me.'

'But you must have some inkling?'

'Well, it is written in a type of Coptic script.'

'What's that?' Anna inquired.

'Ancient Egyptian writing had several evolutions. Initially, there was Hieroglyphics and Hieratic script.'

'Yeah. I've seen Hieroglyphics on obelisks and whatnot.'

'Right. But there was also the more cursive form called Hieratic. Religious texts were written with this. Then came an even more cursive form called Demotic. It was a kind of shorthand that scribes used for more mundane things. But it was exceedingly difficult to learn. Eventually, that started to fall out of favour as Greek was preferred. As the Ancient Egyptian civilisation faded, another form had started. This was an effort to write the native Egyptian words in a phonetic way. Using both Demotic and Greek signs. This was the start of the Coptic script. It …,' Michael hesitated, transfixed by Anna's intense gaze.

He coughed sharply and then continued, 'It was a form of writing that evolved over centuries and only became standardized in the 4th century.'

'So what's on your papyrus?'

'My papyrus?'

'Yes,' she nodded seriously.

'I'm not sure. There are Greek characters and some unusual Demotic ones, so it hints of a very early development.' Anna frowned, obviously analysing what he'd just told her. 'Frank thinks it's a fake. Someone has lifted characters from different texts and mashed them together.'

'Well. What do you think, Michael?'

'To be honest, I really don't know.'

Chapter 7

Oxfordshire, England, present day

The two men stood in the middle of the bridge watching the sculls slice through the water below, the narrow boats leaving knife-like wakes in their path. Rain threatened from the west and the air was damp and cold. Frank had agreed to meet the thin man at this remote location. It all seemed rather paranoid, but the man he was meeting was incredibly private if not extremely wealthy. He wasn't really sure what to think of him: partner, benefactor or employer? When he had first been introduced to him many years before, he had given Mr Smith as his name. But Frank had a suspicion that it wasn't his real one, so he rarely used it. It just added to the drama.

'How was the Nile Valley?' Frank enquired, breaking the silence.

'Nothing of any significance. I really thought there might have been something at Akhmim. But the monastery's archives had been cleared out many years ago.'

Frank knew that the thin man was searching for anything controversial — some new discovery about religion that would change the status quo: a lost book or some secret knowledge only for the benefit of special initiates. The interest in unorthodox theories had ballooned out of all proportion and the hunt was on to find any evidence that supported such outlandish claims.

Frank slowly shook his head. 'As time passes, the chance of new discoveries fade. The most important finds have typically come from documents that were discarded because of faults when they were copied. Kept initially to reuse the parchment and then completely forgotten about. Pushed to the back of some ancient storeroom.' He left the parapet of the bridge and faced his companion. 'Maybe it's time to retire from this game.'

Smith didn't respond to this. Instead he asked, 'How about your end?'

'More of the usual. Though I found an interesting Greek text but it was too brief and too fragmented. I was initially thinking it might be from the Secret Book of James. Some of the phrases bore a close similarity.'

'Frank, you are my eyes and ears in Oxford,' the thin man stated. 'But what I am searching for is more than the contradictory mysticism of the

Gnostics. Their texts are ambiguous and for the most part, too well known.'

Gnosticism was a religious idea that sprang up in the first few centuries of the first millennium. It was a blend of early Christian teaching and Jewish mysticism and led to a variety of schisms in the early Church. Many of these texts were attributed to famous biblical figures to boost their authenticity. Over a hundred different writings had so far been found, which attested to their popularity at the time.

A silence descended on the pair. Each one lost in his own thoughts. The ground mist swirled around the river bank and the surroundings were momentarily lost to view.

'Michael found an Egyptian papyrus last week. It included the name Simon Kanai,' Frank quietly stated after a while.

'The Zealot?'

'Mmm.'

'An intriguing character. Named just once in three of the Gospels and then never mentioned again.' The thin man looked at Frank with a quizzical expression. 'You did keep it safe? Can you show me?'

Frank shook his head. 'It was written in Egyptian and Aramaic. A hoax. A forgery if ever I saw one.'

Smith grunted. Frank responded indignantly, 'You know about the text of Jesus' wife.'

Within the last few years, a fragment of papyrus had surfaced that had garnered widespread attention. Written in a late Coptic dialect, it had made reference to Jesus being married. However, its provenance was questionable and after testing, the dating of the papyrus was found to be medieval.

'Frank, I must insist you tell me if anything like this passes across your desk. Need I remind you of our deal? You have more to lose than I do.'

For several years, Smith had been surreptitiously funding much of the budget of the Registry, allowing Frank to secure its future and resist its amalgamation with other departments. But there was a quid pro quo.

Frank appeared to grow confused, 'Alright. I'll admit that I might have been a bit hasty in dismissing it. But Egyptian …?'

Smith frowned. 'Yes. Well. The Romans banished trouble-makers to the more inhospitable outposts of their Empire. Egypt included. There was the Galilean uprising of 48AD. That was dealt with less harshly than the Great Jewish Revolt of 67, I believe. It's not totally beyond the realm of possibility that the Romans exiled the Zealot there.'

Smith tapped his fingers on the stone casing of the bridge. 'Where is the papyrus now?'

Eventually, Frank replied, 'Michael has it. He thought I wouldn't notice him taking it. But he is on his way to America with a girl.'

The thin man rolled his eyes. 'With the document?' Frank forced a grimace but said nothing. A flock of black-backed gulls skittered across the pale sky, their sharp cries momentarily breaking the calm.

'We need to nip this in the bud. Where are they heading?'

'Their flight is to Phoenix.'

'I know someone there.' Smith took out his cell phone and after a minute of scrolling through the contacts, put it to his ear. 'Alex? Some people need to be watched. Can you do it?'

Chapter 8

London, England and Tucson, USA, present day

The train rattled its way through the drab suburbs of another gloomy town. Rain fell in thick sheets, droplets cascading across the carriage window. As Michael stared through the glass, he couldn't decide whether or not he had made the right decision. He was following Anna back to Arizona. All he knew was that there was no return to what was before. The future was unknown yet exciting. On the other hand, Michael felt guilty taking the fragment without Frank knowing. The papyrus fascinated him more than it warranted, as most of the Egyptian words made little sense.

'Look,' Anna had said the day after her encounter with Frank. 'I used to work in the Mass Spectrometry Department. We used to run dating tests all the time. Come back with me and I'll do it for you. You'll find out in a day or two whether it really does come from the distant past or if it's a recent forgery.'

'No, no. I don't want to destroy the papyrus.'

'That's in the past now. We don't need that much material anymore. Just a milligram or so.'

'What? I thought you had to cut up a beer mat sized portion.'

'Not now.' Anna drew out the last word. 'We use Accelerator Mass Spectrometry. It uses all the radioactive carbon atoms in the sample, not just the ones undergoing decay. So, you need much less.'

'Frank won't like it,' Michael said.

Anna threw up her arms in exasperation, 'Why does he even have to know?'

So, Michael had packed a bag, asked Frank for a week off and booked a seat on the same returning flight as Anna. Frank was a little suspicious at first, but Michael hinted that it involved the girl. He thought Frank kind of got the message. Frank even told him to take a fortnight off as Michael hadn't actually taken any leave in the past two years.

The train terminated in London at Paddington station and they took the underground out to the airport. It was early. Their departure time was around noon, so they had taken the first train from Oxford. The rain had stopped, but the sky was grey and streaked with ragged clouds.

People on the tube were grim faced and quiet. Even though the morning rush hour was coming to an end, the carriage was still quite packed. Michael couldn't help but see the consequences of lives left ordinary. Passions dulled by the endless routine of the daily rhythm.

They passed through check-in and immigration without any hitch and boarded the plane on time. During the flight, Michael questioned Anna on her previous work and why she chose to be a scientist. He had read somewhere that girls liked being asked questions and decided to give it a go.

'I grew up believing that the Universe was like a mechanical watch,' she had expounded. 'Intricate yet fundamentally explainable. I soon realised this view was flawed. Our explanations are only approximate. There are many physical values that define our Universe: the speed of light, the charge on an electron and so on. But there are twenty-six special ones that all the others can be derived from. Why do they have the exact values that they do have? Nobody knows. We do know that if they were even slightly different, then our world would differ greatly from the one we recognize today. Change one, the Fine Structure Constant, by a few percent and there would be no carbon in the cosmos. Hence, no life. That constant has a value of one over one hundred and thirty-seven. One of the really great physicists of our time said, 'The hand of God wrote that number but we don't know how he pushed his pencil'.'

Anna drew up her legs and swivelled in her seat to face him. 'So, I chose to be a scientist because this is the only field I can ask these questions and hopefully find answers.' Her eyes were dark and intense as she said this. Then they brightened, and a grin appeared on her face. 'Also, it's pretty cool playing with all the expensive toys we have.'

Shortly afterwards, having evidently exhausted herself with this answer, she fell asleep for the rest of the flight. As the plane dropped down through the clouds over Phoenix, she woke, yawned and mumbled, 'My friend is picking us up from the airport. We'll crash at her place tonight. I'll sort out something more permanent tomorrow.'

Coming from the cool wet climate of Oxford, Michael felt overwhelmed by the dry heat of Arizona. The drive to Tucson took them south from Phoenix through dry, patchy scrubland. Anna's friend, Sarah, lived in a two-storey house with a flat roof and wide windows — a squat block at the end of a dusty lane, not far from the Rillito River.

Anna and Michael took turns showering, and they spent the remaining part of the day picking up new SIM cards before jet lag forced them to the sanctuary of sleep. Just before his eyelids closed for the last time, Michael heard Sarah quietly strumming an acoustic guitar outside and singing an old Leonard Cohen song to herself.

A honeyed light greeted them the following morning and doused the place with warm shadows, the air cool and brittle. After breakfast, Sarah dropped Anna and Michael off downtown and they walked to the University of Arizona, its low-rise buildings surrounded by palm and olive trees. The campus was centred on a long stretch of open ground the students called the Mall and was framed by a ring of tan-coloured mountains in the distance.

Initially, they criss-crossed the university grounds sorting out the administration associated with Anna's return: a new identity badge, library access card, medical insurance forms and finally booking some accommodation in one of the campus dormitories for both of them.

'Alright. The test will take a few days to prep and do. You won't be allowed in the lab. They are pretty uptight about that. But it's a term break so it'll be quiet and I can do it without any interruptions,' Anna said authoritatively.

'What am I going to do?' Michael said, not entirely happy about this.

'Well …' Eventually, Anna convinced Michael to sit in on a few basic particle physics courses, all part of a summer school. 'You'll like this Professor. And you will need more insight into my world if we are going to spend more time together,' she said, coyly.

So shortly afterwards, Michael found himself in a cavernous auditorium, hoping that no one would ask him any questions. The other students, freshmen Anna had said, looked so much older than him, even though they were probably at least four years younger.

The black-haired lecturer slouched against the bench at the front of the theatre. His eyes were dark and brooding — a rock star scientist, Michael thought. As soon as the doors at the back closed, he thrust out his hands and, with a rich sonorous voice, proclaimed, 'There is a storm. A hailstorm of particles slicing through our bodies.' He paused and visibly checked himself.

'No, hailstorm is the wrong word. There is no rain on Earth that can match that which passes through our flesh, every second of every day, for our whole life. A hundred thousand billion every second.' He waited a minute for effect.

'I talk of neutrinos. Particles born in the sun. An essential part of the nuclear processes that turns matter into energy. But ghost particles. They have no charge and are a billion times smaller than an electron.' And so, he went on, delivering knowledge like it was essential to life. Michael was impressed.

Lectures on other fundamental particles followed throughout the next few days and Michael began to understand why Anna was so fascinated by the field. These were God's building blocks — immutable, immortal and set in motion for eternity. Actually, Michael realised that this was a question he could ask Anna. Do atoms ever wear out? Surely, they can't go rushing about forever without sickening, he thought.

The last day of the week was ending and the setting sun was turning the university buildings gloriously gold. Michael sat on one of the benches scattered around the grounds near the Faculty of Science. Here he had waited for Anna every evening until she had finished her tasks for the day.

He was so mesmerised by the changing colours of the sky that he did not notice her approaching until she called out his name.

'Michael. Michael from Oxford,' she repeated with a laugh.

He looked up at her with clear delight, instinctively reaching up to touch her hand. She sat down next to him. 'Well, it's done. I got the data.'

'What does it say?' Michael's thoughts instantly switched to the papyrus. He could hardly contain his anticipation.

'Look. The sample was on the small size. I only used the barest amount. A few pieces from one of the flaking edges. Right on the limit of usability. Seventy-five micrograms of carbon.'

'Yes. Yes. The result?'

'It's not enough to be absolutely certain.'

'I understand, I understand. What date?'

'50AD. Plus or minus 60 years.'

Chapter 9

Tucson, USA, present day

The campus café was packed with students and staff the following morning. A bright blue sky and crisp clean air heralded the day as Anna and Michael stood in line to get coffee and pastries.

'You sure you want to go ahead with this?' Anna asked. The thought had more than once disturbed Michael's sleep during the night. 'We go with a larger piece?' She had explained that with a bigger sample the date could be pinned down more accurately. Also, she was going to involve one of her professors to make it all legitimate and above reproach.

'In for a penny, in for a pound,' was all Michael could answer her.

She looked at him quizzically. 'What?'

Then he noticed the other students staring back across the Mall. He twisted around to look in that direction. A tall column of smoke drifted up into the sky. Almost immediately there was the wail of sirens and people started to scatter. Michael turned back towards Anna, but she was already pushing through the crowd towards the door.

The four-storey building that housed the AMS laboratory was wreathed in a grey haze. Yellow-suited fire crew were already hosing down the roof by the time they arrived. A few campus security guards had also appeared and began moving onlookers back from the building. Loud crackling and the occasional sharp pop sounded incongruously in the almost perfect cobalt morning.

Anna turned to Michael, slightly breathless from their run across the lawn, her face ashen with worry. 'Shit. Suspicion will fall on me.'

'What do you mean?'

'I was the only one working in the lab this week.

'Look, it's not your fault.'

'Apart from the visiting lecturer who popped in yesterday, I was the only one there. I'm going to be screwed over this. Do you have any idea just how much all that equipment cost?'

They hung around for most of the day, watching the firemen douse the last smouldering embers and tape off the building. Several lecturers and administration staff gathered near a couple of policemen, who were asking them questions and taking notes.

By late afternoon, Anna had fallen into a sullen silence. She continuously chewed her bottom lip and paced incessantly. At one point, she got to talk to another research assistant who knew more details. Only the AMS laboratory had been affected, but luckily no one was inside. However, it had been totally gutted. Once he had gone, Michael tried to reassure her that it would be alright — that no one was hurt, but she just flashed him a look.

'Will you just stop? You don't know what this will do to me.'

'No one's going to blame you.'

Then it suddenly occurred to Michael. The papyrus piece was in the laboratory. Anna had insisted it be kept in a dehumidifier cabinet whilst they decided what to do.

'You left the fragment inside?' Michael asked — a little sharply.

Anna twisted to glare at him and then shook her head once. 'I have to go now.' She picked up her bag and was gone, disappearing into the crowd. It seemed so sudden and he didn't react immediately. He looked at the people nearby, all strangers. Some stared back with indifference and a feeling of loss suddenly gripped him.

He waited until sunset, but Anna didn't return. Her cell phone was switched off and his calls went straight to voice mail. Michael hurried back to her dormitory. She wasn't there either.

Anna didn't show up that night or all of the next day. Michael walked around the campus, going from cafeteria to the lab to the dorm, but still didn't see her. Michael really started to worry now. He cursed himself for being too blunt. He was coming to realise that not all questions were good.

That evening, Michael ended up on a bus stop bench, feeling alone and a bit sorry for himself. It felt like he had been given a gift which had then been rudely snatched away. Trams rattled past every few minutes, the ground rumbling with their passage. Across the road from him was a brick-built warehouse complex that had been redeveloped as a nightspot. Groups of young people strolled along the broad pavement, laughing and cavorting at the end of the day.

On impulse, Michael stood up and crossed the street. The bar was dimly lit and crowded. He hesitated and wondered if this was going to help, before pushing the door open and walking inside. He ordered a beer and took the only available seat at the counter. Ordinarily, Michael was good at planning, weighing up his options and figuring out what he should do next. But he felt like he was in unchartered territory, a fog dulling his wits.

The man seated next to Michael at the bar was ordering another drink. Then he turned to Michael and asked, 'You look like you could do with another. What'll it be?'

Normally, Michael would refuse such an offer, but now he just held up his bottle. 'Thanks,' he accepted.

The man was an out-of-towner too. Here in Tucson for some exhibition, alone and with his own personal turmoil like Michael. 'Made too many mistakes in my life, you know,' he quietly confessed moments later. Michael had to admit, he wasn't really paying attention to what the man was saying. How to get back in touch with Anna preoccupied his mind.

Michael then became aware that the man had stopped talking. He realized that he might have taken offence to the absence of any attention.

Michael looked over and saw he was just staring into his drink. But then the man murmured to him, 'Who's in your life?'

'Just Frank really,' Michael responded, slightly relieved.

'Frank. He your dad.'

'No. My dad's dead. I work with Frank. He was my father's friend.'

'What about your mother?'

'I'm not sure.'

'What do you mean, you're not sure? How does one lose one's mother?'

'She left when I was younger. Maybe when I was fifteen or so.'

'What happened?'

It had been so long ago that Michael didn't immediately know how to answer the man. He picked up on the hesitation.

'It's okay, my friend. You don't need to answer.'

'No. I just try not to think about it much.' His father had once mentioned that there was another man involved. Michael had come back from school and found she had gone — no note, no explanation.

'Trust me, friend. You have to hang on to those you want to walk your life with,' his companion slurred before laying his head on his folded arms.

On his way back to the dormitory, Michael found a bicycle outside the Administration Building that wasn't chained up. In a moment of clarity, he decided to cycle the five miles out to the apartment of Anna's friend, near the river. She was the only other person he knew on this continent. Sarah opened the door on a chain at first, before closing and reopening it completely when she recognised him. However, she didn't ask Michael inside and he stood forlornly on the doorstep.

'Hello, Sarah. Have you seen Anna?'

'Not recently. Why, what's the matter?'

'Something happened at the lab. She took off and now she's disappeared.' Michael's stomach knotted when he said this.

Sarah didn't respond immediately. No alarm or worry showed on her face, which somehow didn't seem right to him. Then Michael noticed a book lying on the chair next to the porch. It was one Anna had been reading over the past few days. 'She's here. This is Anna's.'

'No. No, she's not.'

'But you know where she is?'

'Sorry Michael. I'm not sure what to say to you. She got a message from the Dean saying she was suspended until they find out what happened. The University is waiting to hear back from the Tucson Fire Department.'

'Do you know where she is?' Michael repeated.

Sarah started to shake her head but then smiled slightly and put a finger to her lips.

'Look, I shouldn't really tell you but she's gone back to her parents.' Michael stared at her, willing her to carry on. 'Sedona. It's a place north of here.' She wrote an address on the back of an old receipt. 'Here, I didn't tell you. Okay?'

Chapter 10

Sedona, USA, present day

It is two hundred and thirty miles and about five hours from Tucson to Sedona. The information booth at the coach station on East 12th Street was Michael's first stop. Getting a Greyhound to Phoenix was fine, but Sedona was another matter. He resigned himself to getting the bus to Flagstaff and getting off near Lake Montezuma, then hitching a ride into Sedona.

North of Phoenix, the landscape was barren and empty. Long plains of sandstone and gravel stretched to the horizon. This is what Mars must look like, Michael thought. Without the cacti, though. The bus pulled into a truck stop on the I-17 and he soon found an eighteen-wheeler going through Oak Creek Canyon on its way north. The grey-bearded driver was more than happy to reunite him with 'his girl'.

Half an hour later, the carriage-way began to climb and after a while crested a rise. Salmon-red rocks rose either side of the road — low at first, but soon they towered over the truck. Before long, Michael was surrounded by rust-coloured cliffs and escarpments that marched off into the distance.

After passing over a bridge on the edge of town, the truck came to a stop near a massive gas station. 'This is it, Bud,' smiled the trucker. Slinging his duffle bag onto his shoulder, Michael stepped down to the baked ground and saluted the grizzled man. The driver winked at him, then gunned the engine and coaxed his truck back onto the road.

Surprisingly, there was no one around, the pumps all empty. Michael walked across the forecourt to the payment kiosk. A woman in a blue uniform was pricing up cans of soda. 'What can I do for you, hon?' She looked at him with a cheerful expression.

'I'm looking for this address,' Michael held out Sarah's scribbled note.

'Well, let me see. That's about three miles out of town. You turn off onto West Canyon Road and it's down there aways.'

By the time Michael reached the wooden gate, the sky had already turned indigo. Out front of the low ranch-style house, a man was lifting bales of hay onto a pickup. He turned to Michael as soon as Michael pushed the gate open. 'What is it, son?' The man had a rich mellow voice, immediately welcoming.

'I am Michael. I'm looking for Anna.'

'You the boy from England? She knows you're comin'?' Michael shook his head. 'How'd you get here? You walk from town?'

'Yeah,' Michael nodded.

'Ah. Well, she is out at her special place. She took the bike. It's down through the woods there and you follow the track up the hill.' Michael stared at him, not completely sure what he should do. The man looked him up and down and shrugged, evidently concluding Michael was harmless. 'Come on, I'll take you to her.' He fired up a quad bike parked in front of the house, gestured for him to climb on the back and they shot off down the path.

The trip was a rush for Michael, down dirt banks and across shallow rock-strewn streams, water arcing in sheets either side of them. The bike finally pushed through a stand of mesquite bushes. 'Anna!' the driver called out.

'Dad?'

'Someone to see ya.'

Anna was standing on a slab of rock that projected out into space. The rocks, and even the very earth, were a rich red sienna. A few gnarled trees framed the small summit and parked beside one was a beat-up dirt bike. She looked at Michael with what he assumed to be exasperation. Michael got down and walked over to her. She looked over his shoulder. 'It's okay, Dad. I'll bring him back. You don't need to wait.' He nodded to her and turned the four-wheeler around.

Once he had gone, Michael spoke. 'Why did you come here?'

'To think.' She walked back to the rock outcrop and gazed off into the distance. 'A number of places around here are sacred to the Native Americans. People travel from faraway to visit these spots and become … rejuvenated. Me, I just like the peace of the place.'

'You're safe. That's good.' Michael couldn't tell whether or not she was angry with him. Uncertain whether he should approach her, he stood off to one side. A cool wind started to pick up and ruffled Anna's hair, her expression unfathomable.

Michael wasn't sure what to say next. He began to apologize, words that he had rehearsed a hundred times on the journey here, but Anna hushed him before he completed a single sentence. She had turned to face him now. 'Before I met you, my life was simple. All logic and reason. Black and white, really. You have fucked that up.'

A frown appeared on her forehead. 'I like you, Michael. But all the time I know … I know, there is this.' Her arms swept across the sky. 'Challenging me to aspire to its precision. Its perfectness.' At this point, night had fallen completely with a deep inky blackness. The sky seethed with stars and a milky slash swept southwards. 'There is a cold and complicated universe wheeling across this earthly mess. Glorious in its beauty and indifference. And I am reminded of it at night, in the dark.'

Michael could barely make out her face now, but her voice continued coolly, 'It's not that I don't want to be with you. I just see most things as inconsequential to this.' Michael's heart sank, and he was momentarily unable to think. Anna continued, 'After the fire at the lab, I convinced myself it was the wrong time and the wrong

71

place. I thought there was something that was more important than us.'

'Then … is there no place for me?' Michael finally asked.

She walked over to Michael and to his complete surprise enfolded him in her arms. The simple action made his legs weaken. 'I have thought about it. I guess I blamed you for something that wasn't your fault.'

They stood hugging for several minutes. Michael, reluctant to let the moment pass, finally spoke, 'I would like to finish what has been started. But I don't want to do it without you,' he whispered.

She looked at him with her gentle blue eyes. 'I'm not sure if there is anything more to do. But whatever there is, I guess we can do it together. Is that all right?'

They returned back to the house, Anna gunning the dirt bike slowly down the track. Once they got there, she pulled him towards the front door. 'Come on, you need to be properly introduced to my parents. Then you need to wash,' she wrinkled up her nose. 'I guess you've not changed for a few days.' She glanced at Michael and soberly voiced, 'Thank you for coming to find me.'

The admission was disarming but he couldn't resist replying, 'I'm not sure you were lost.' Anna's face was about to explode, then she saw his quiet smile and smacked his arm. Michael grinned even more. 'It's alright. I know what you meant.'

Later, after dinner, Michael watched Anna and her parents tidy away and envied the obvious affection between them. The house was seductively lit with pools of golden light strategically illuminating the table, bookshelf, and kitchen counter. It was warm and welcoming. The food had been good too, wholesome and lots of it. At that moment, sitting in front of the log fire, Michael felt his eyelids droop and his head dip.

To shrug off the feeling of tiredness that now ambushed him, Michael reached out and pulled on his canvas bag. The handle snagged on a chair and fell, its contents fanning out across the floor. 'Bugger!' he grumbled.

Michael knelt down and started to gather the books and things together. A cream-coloured envelope poked out from the paperback he had been reading on the plane — the very envelope that had contained the papyrus. Forgetting the bag, Michael drew it out and stared at the writing. Slowly, he began to decipher the terrible scrawl. The most obvious word was the last one, 'Roma.'

Chapter 11

Oxford, England, present day

'It's gone. Apparently.'

'Amateurs!' exclaimed Frank. 'They destroyed the very thing we wanted.'

'They were just trying to find out what the boy had discovered. If you hadn't let him take it away in the first place …' Smith's voice trailed off.

'Okay. Okay. You don't have to keep rubbing it in.'

Smith eyed Frank reproachfully. 'Well, you had better keep your feelings in check. I've flown them over to meet us.'

'What!' Frank spluttered.

'Yes. We need their … energy.'

Frank and the thin man walked past large display cases and in a quiet corner came across two men, standing languidly against a wall. They were in the main hall of Oxford's Natural History Museum, giant dinosaur skeletons towering above them. Both had close cropped hair and beards, and wore boots, jeans and windbreakers. They were young but had creased eyes and weathered faces.

'Hello gentlemen! This is Alex and he is Gethan,' Smith introduced them to Frank.

'Yeah. Hi. You're not pissed about Arizona?' The one called Alex spoke.

'A little. But let's move on from that.'

'What happened?' Frank insisted, not willing to let it go.

Alex replied, 'I managed to get in the lab.'

'Lab?' Frank turned around sharply.

'Yeah. The carbon dating lab.'

'Michael was dating the document?'

'Seems so. Well, the girl was.'

Frank looked at the thin man, flummoxed. 'I don't get it.'

'Alex followed them to the university in Tucson. The girl was working in the Mass Spectrometry Lab for a few days, so he gained access and snooped around for a bit.'

'That's right,' Alex grunted. 'I don't understand what she was doin' exactly. But when she was out one time, I flicked through her notes. There was a chart with a curve and dates along the bottom. She had drawn a line down from the curve. Whatever it was, it was old, man. Around two thousand years old.' Frank and Smith shared a glance. 'But as I was leavin', I knocked over a flask. It fizzled and gave off this white smoke, so I scarpered.'

'Damn it!' Frank cursed. 'I'd never seen anything like that papyrus. It just didn't seem right. I couldn't think of any conceivable situation that Old Coptic could be linked to Aramaic.'

'The time periods don't overlap?' the thin man asked.

'No. It would make more sense if it was written in common Greek or even standard Coptic. Some of the glyphs were familiar but others were … It just seemed so obviously …'

'Primitive. A way of writing that was developing?' finished Smith.

'What do ya mean?' Gethan asked. It was the first time he had spoken.

The thin man continued, 'Writing in Egypt during the first century was an assortment of many forms. Demotic was used side by side with Greek. But a new script was developing as a combination of the two. It went through numerous variations until it settled on a more standardised version in the fourth century. This became what is known as Coptic.'

'However, initially it was very idiosyncratic. There was no one common decision on which Demotic characters were used for sounds that didn't exist in the Greek alphabet. That fact alone would mean it was older. How did I miss it?' muttered Frank.

'Just as well I lifted it then,' smirked Alex.

'You have it?' Smith asked sharply.

'Yeah. It's in my nature to nick everything. I saw it in a glass cabinet and took it.'

'What's it worth?' Gethan asked.

'If it's real, it could be priceless. But even if it's a fake, it could still be worth something.'

'What do ya mean priceless?' Gethan's face lit up.

'Well, the Ryland's Papyrus is the oldest Gospel fragment known to exist,' said Smith. 'Most experts date it to around the mid-second century. But like most rare documents, it is part of a university collection. They don't come onto the market. But a third century fragment was sold for half a million dollars not long ago.' Alex whistled.

'The dating only confirms the papyrus material was old. It could still be a forgery.'

'A forgery?' Gethan enquired, his face frowning at the statement.

'Yes. You can take an old papyrus with worthless text, chemically wash off the ink and rewrite whatever you want.'

'But that doesn't make sense. Who would go to all the trouble of preparing it and then leave it sitting in an obscure storeroom in Oxford for who knows how long?' Frank fired back.

'Where is it?' Smith questioned Alex.

'Safe. For now.' He swaggered a little and pointed a finger at the two older men. 'I feel we have been a bit peripheral to your cause. I'm thinking we might be … promoted as it were.'

Chapter 12

Rome, Italy, present day

The Mercedes that dropped Anna and Michael off on the secluded street near the main train station of Rome had seen better days. But the ride-sharing fare had been substantially cheaper than getting a taxi from the airport. The Italian student who had accompanied them to the city centre was obviously shy, spoke little and the first to get out.

Buildings in pastel hues edged the street. The road was completely lined with parked cars and scooters. A few dogs wandered along the pavement, but other than that, it was empty.

'This is it,' Michael declared.

'The address on the envelope?' Anna responded.

'Yes. I think so. Number 17. Addressed to a Marietta Larusso.' A tall modern building with a grey brick façade and large glass windows occupied the whole block. 'This can't be right.' Michael walked down the street a bit and then returned to Anna.

She pointed to some numbers etched into one of the glass panes. 'Numero 11–19.' Below this was the name of an Italian architectural company. 'It doesn't exist anymore,' she said calmly. 'They must have redeveloped it. There's only this office here now.'

'Fuck,' was all Michael could say.

'How old was that letter?' Anna asked.

'I think it was written about the time of the Second World War.'

'What? Seventy years ago.' She rolled her eyes.

'But they never knock anything down in Italy.'

'You hoped,' she quipped.

Nearby, rubbish bins were pushed up against the wall. They were overflowing with cardboard boxes and the leftover remains of what must have been a fruit stall. Over-ripe peaches and mangoes littered the area and a sweet sickly smell pervaded the air. Anna covered her nose, took Michael's arm and pulled him down the street towards a piazza. 'Let's get away from here. And get some food.'

The square at the end of the road was tree-lined and shady, and on the far side was a classic Italian café. Cast-iron chairs and tables spilled out onto the wide stone pavement. Waiters in black with white aprons hustled trays of drinks and plates of food to the seated customers.

'Here. Let's eat out here,' Anna said as they squeezed through the packed place and grabbed the last remaining table outside. After a few slices of pizza and several cups of coffee, they still hadn't spoken much. At last, Michael pushed his plate away, opened up a map of Rome and folded it to the district of San Lorenzo. He peered at the small writing, hoping to find some mistake he had made or a clue he had missed. Finally, Michael gave up and mumbled, 'A dead end, I guess.'

Anna viewed him sympathetically. 'Well, it was the only lead we had left. What should we do now?'

'Have you heard back from your university?' Michael interjected.

'No. No decision. Just that there is a review and it will take a week or two to process all the evidence. I sent them my side of the story when I was back home in Sedona.' She forced a smile and professed, 'No point worrying about it. What do you say about exploring the city?' The thought of several days in Rome with Anna was sounding pretty good to Michael. He started to refold the map.

'Scusi, my son. Where do you want to go?' An elderly man in a brown suit had turned in his seat to look at them.

'No. No. I'm not going anywhere. I wanted to find this address. But all I have found is a new building. I was expecting something older.' Michael pointed at the street location.

'Let me see, young man?' He took out a pair of silver-rimmed glasses from his jacket pocket.

'I have this letter and I wanted to find out who lived there.'

The old man did something with his mouth, a kind of pout, as he squinted at the map. 'You know this whole area was bombed during the war. Many houses were destroyed. Those that survived were relocated. That side of the street took a direct hit.' He took a handkerchief from his jacket pocket and dabbed his forehead. 'Those were terrible times. Good times, too. When you could trust your neighbours. Leave your doors unlocked. People looked out for each other.'

Michael was wondering how to make some excuse and leave. The old man was clearly nostalgic.

'Who are you looking for?' came the wavering voice.

Michael hesitated and looked at the envelope. 'A Marietta Larusso. But she might have lived there some time ago.' Anna sarcastically nodded her head in agreement.

The old man thought for a while, 'No. I don't know of any Marietta.'

'Oh, well. Thank you.' Michael started to shove the map into his bag.

'But there is a family Larusso living in the next street over. Number 54, I believe. Maybe they would know who she was?'

Number 54 was a tall terraced house with a wide entrance that opened into a small courtyard. Willowy trees with silver branches stood in pots along the sides and a stone staircase rose to the second storey.

'Hallo,' Michael called out. But there was no reply. He walked to the bottom of the stairs and peered up. A small boy of about ten appeared at the top and stared at them over the parapet. 'Mamma e Papà?' Michael asked him.

The boy shook his head.

'Nessuno?' Michael turned to Anna and explained, 'I'm asking if there is anyone else.'

'Nonna.' The boy pointed to the third level.

'Right, let's go up,' Michael muttered.

The boy proceeded to lead them up another flight of stairs and into a small cluttered room with sliding windows which opened onto a wide terracotta-tiled terrace.

He pushed open the glass door and indicated with his chin, the white-haired lady sitting on a wooden chair in the corner. Her pale watery eyes turned to them as they walked out onto the balcony. They could see that the terrace looked out over the tan-coloured rooftops of Rome, towards the snow-tinged mountains of the Apennines. It was incredibly beautiful. Michael regretted that he hadn't visited the city before now.

'Madame Marietta?' he enquired.

He prepared himself to speak to her in Italian, but the old lady replied in heavily accented but quite understandable English, 'Who are you?'

'My name is Michael. This is Anna,' Michael pointed at Anna as a way of introduction. 'I was given this old envelope. It is addressed to a Marietta Larusso. It has what looks like an Egyptian stamp on it. Do you think it could be you?' Michael offered it to the elderly woman.

She gazed at him for some time, before taking the envelope from his outstretched hand. 'No. No. It's not me.'

Michael's heart sank. But he guessed it was to be expected. 'Then we are sorry to disturb you.' He gave her a weak smile. He wanted to say something more but couldn't think of anything other than, 'Your English is excellent.'

'Yes. I was a school teacher. I taught English at a girl's school near Perugia. I loved teaching. I loved books. Poetry was my favourite.' Her voice faltered, and she looked down at the object in her hands. Finally, she sighed. 'This was for my mother.' She stroked the envelope with her frail fingers. Then she added, 'And it was my father who wrote this address.'

Chapter 13

Rome, Italy, present day

The white-haired woman rocked slightly as she began. 'I will tell you, as my father told me thirty years ago. I remember as if it was yesterday. He was already quite old, well past sixty when I travelled out to see him for the last time. By then, he was living outside Rome, in the country. The scene replays over and over again in my head.'

The old lady then told her story, her eyes unwavering, as they saw into the past — the bus pulling back onto the road, veiled in dust and rattling with decrepitude — the cloud settling. Picking up her bag and walking up the path to the farmhouse.

Crossing the courtyard, she had entered through an open door. In the kitchen sat an aged man who gazed through the window to the garden beyond. 'It seems to me that every time I come, you are expecting someone,' the woman said.

'Hope is an old man's curse.' The sadness in the eyes of Assistant-Profosorre Arturo Morretti of the

Istituto di Archeologia di Roma said much to his daughter.

'Papà? You have to tell me. Mamma won't say anything. I have no idea why she won't speak to you.'

A coarse cough and a kind of animal shudder initiated his confession. A final resignation, as if here was a release of everything that had held his life in check, up until that moment.

'This! It was this,' he said. Pulling open the drawer, he drew a leather book out and flung it onto the tabletop. 'I so wanted to be recognised. To be something more than ... what I was. And still ...' He left the sentence unfinished. 'Oh daughter. If only things had been different. Surely it would have been better.' He pulled a cloth from his jacket and wiped his face. His daughter could see that he was unable to control his tears. 'Scusa,' he said, his voice muffled by the handkerchief, and he stumbled out of the room.

Back in the present, the elderly woman's eyes seemed to refocus, and she looked up at Anna and Michael. 'And so he left me to read his journal.'

She took out a small brass key and reached over to a wooden box resting on the table next to her. Taking her time, she unlocked it and drew from it a dark leather-bound book. 'Here. It is best you read it, just like I did thirty years ago,' the old lady said. Passing it over to Michael, she slowly got up from the chair and walked to the balcony door. Without a word, she went inside.

Anna came over to Michael and together they sat on a wide wooden bench and he carefully opened the cover. Copious notes and drawings filled the cream-coloured pages. What looked like the layouts of buildings were interspersed with diagrams of archaic parchments. Then towards the back and bookmarked by a thin brown ribbon were several pages of a neat handwritten text — written in English.

Chapter 14

Dear Eva,

The road to Siwa was a long one. In writing this, I mean not only was it a considerable effort to get there but the whole affair has consumed my life. I am old now, but I was a young man when I first walked on the sands of Egypt.

Even now, I remember it quite well, arriving at Siwa just before sunset — seeing the oasis for the first time after the long bus ride from the coast. Stepping down onto the bare earth and looking up into the sky and seeing the thousands of birds perched on the branches of the Eucalyptus trees. The air was full of their song. What a magical place it seemed.

The reason for my journey was the scrap of parchment I kept between the covers of my notebook. Innocuous, almost worthless it seemed — the size of my palm and brown like an autumn leaf with black scratchings rather than words upon it.

In my youth, I was poor and yet I dreamt of finding some wonderful ancient treasure. I wanted to be honoured amongst the great people of the world. In my free time, I would scrabble in the dirt by the ruins of the Coliseum. When I was sixteen, an exhibition of the pharaohs came to Rome. I was enthralled by the great sculptures and magnificent artifacts. It became my ambition to see this faraway land, which seemingly had thousands of relics just waiting to be unearthed.

I badgered my parents, who eventually relented and got me enrolled at the Institute of Archaeology in Rome. However, it wasn't until 1938 that I left Italy for Egypt. I was a junior assistant on a dig just outside Faiyum, seventy miles south of Cairo. It wasn't the place I wanted to be, in the middle of nowhere with what ruins that remained in a pitiful state. When the Italian mission in Egypt pulled out because of the declaration of war in Europe, I stayed on. Two British professors came out and took over. They were happy to leave me be and even arranged for me to have a special permit to travel unhindered. I didn't care for the politics of my home country.

It was one day in March 1942 that an Egyptian foreman brought a local to me. He had something to show one of the two professors in charge of the excavation, but both of them were away in Cairo. I took the piece and realised it was of very unusual origin. The fragment was not from the local site, I could see that immediately. It was written in a strange script. The local said his cousin had found several pots, full with such pieces. However, he had been stricken down with malaria and had passed away a few days before. He had lived in the old oasis of Sekht-am — Siwa as it was known locally. I told the man it was worthless, interesting for amateur collectors and I gave him some small notes to keep him happy. Still, I got him to give me his cousin's name. Apparently, the oasis is small and everybody knows everybody else.

It never occurred to me until much later that evening that I could somehow profit from it. Not financially. It was the chance of making a name for myself.

I decided to travel to the oasis in the hope of finding more of the papyri the farmer had uncovered. The fragment is tantalising. It looks strange and unlike anything I have seen before. I informed the senior archaeologist I had to visit Cairo where my brother was sick with fever. This was readily accepted — the whole city is plagued with sickness. However, I could not stay long in Siwa, the journey had already taken me almost a week, and I had to return before I was missed.

After much questioning and baksheesh, I found the location of the dead man's orchard, but the task to find the pots seemed too much for one man. The soil was still crusty after the rain. I surveyed the orchard *and made a map. Every tree and rock I marked. I only hoped that I could come back once I had more time.*

I returned to Cairo and intended to resign my post. I didn't want the two professore claiming my discovery for themselves. But the day after I arrived back in the city, I met your mother, Marietta Larusso, for the first time. She was young, eighteen or so. Even now, a day doesn't go by without a thought of her.

Her family were from Rome also. Their house there was within a stone's throw of the Termini train station. But for many years they had lived in Cairo. Marietta's father, a cotton merchant, like most of the Italian men, had been interned by the British and held in a camp, north of the city. The women had been left to fend for themselves, most in the old Jewish Quarter. But anti-British Egyptian officers helped hide a few men, getting them forged papers and travel documents. I too was helped and for two months I dallied, putting off the inevitable.

One day we walked in the gardens of Zamalek, on the Island of Gezira, and amongst the jasmine, I promised my love to her. We spent that night in each other's arms and made plans for our future together in our home city of Rome.

However, before we could return to Europe, the war suddenly became more serious for us. There was news that the Germans were moving towards Cairo. The sky over the city was turned grey with ash as the British burned documents by the boatload. I saw my grand dream withering in front of me. It could only be saved if I left for Siwa immediately and renew my efforts to find the buried pots. I didn't have time to tell your mother, but I left her a note. I caught the last bus out to Mersa Matruh. It was a nightmare journey through countless military checkpoints. Nevertheless, I reached the oasis on the fourth day.

That night, the Italians bombed the town, and the British pulled out. I hid, for I hadn't found what I had come for. The area was engulfed in flames and bore little resemblance to the place I had visited before. The British had dug up the place for fortifications. The day after, Italian tanks entered the town. The locals were furious at the British for running away. It was touch and go, but I managed to convince the invaders of my Italian nationality. It was a close thing, but a boy from my neighbourhood recognised me and convinced his commander. Young boys from the fascist brigade, they were. I was stuck there for three months wondering how to get back to Cairo.

Then one night, under cover of darkness, I watched a small convoy of trucks enter the old town. They headed directly for the eastern part of the oasis. Groups of green-uniformed men jumped down from the vehicles and set up a perimeter. The German Army had arrived.

I saw that they were still there in the morning, but now there looked as if a coordinated search was going on. A single man seemed to be in charge, directing the careful probing and removal of the top layers of dirt and sand. The next day, I was called to the Command Headquarters. My employment at the Institute of Archaeology had come to the attention of the Germans.

Chapter 15

Siwa, Egypt, 1942

A man in a black uniform sat at the desk in front of Arturo. He was slightly built, with more the appearance of an academic than a soldier. He introduced himself as Standartenführer Ulrich Meyer. Without any preamble, he asked Arturo what he knew of Amun.

'Amun, the ancient Egyptian god?' Arturo replied. 'Well, he rose to become the greatest of the Egyptian deities then faded into obscurity after the twentieth dynasty. He was originally the god of air. The breath of life.'

'Go on,' the German officer encouraged.

'The radical pharaoh Akhenaten deposed all other gods, worshipping Amun as the only one true god whom he renamed, Aten. Even after his cult had waned in Egypt, his priests held great sway outside of the country. In Nubia, his oracles had the power to choose kings, dictate wars and foretell the future. But please, can I ask why the German army is interested in ancient history?'

'I am an investigator with the Berlin Ahnenerbe Institute. We have information that some of the Oracle's revelations have survived!'

'Where?' the Italian asked.

'The Oracle of Amun, here in the oasis of Siwa,' replied Meyer.

The archaeologist pondered this and said, 'Si. The same place to which Alexander the Great travelled after the battle of Issus. To be acknowledged the son of the god and told he would rule the world one day.'

'Which I believe he did. What is more, the Oracle seemed to have the power to destroy armies,' the German continued.

'Are you talking about Cambyses?' Arturo suggested.

'Yes, the Persian king who invaded Egypt. He had been angered by several of its prophecies and decided to destroy the Oracle. So, he sent a large army of fifty thousand men to finish it. They set out from Luxor in Upper Egypt and crossed the desert to the Oasis of Amun. They never arrived. It was many years later that an Ancient Greek historian wrote that the people of the oasis told him the army had been wiped out even before reaching Siwa.'

'But the Temple is in great decay.' Arturo stated. 'There are very few remains of the original complex left standing. There is nothing there.'

'That is what we thought. However, researchers at the Ahnenerbe have recently discovered that in 1798 a German explorer, Frederick Hornemann, travelled in the guise of an Arabic trader to the oasis. He and his interpreter, another German, Joseph Freudenberg, searched the place for eight days. The natives of the oasis were extremely suspicious of any outsiders and prevented him from examining the Temple in detail. But not before he had uncovered some parchments and apparently buried most of them somewhere nearby.'

'I do not understand how this helps,' said Arturo.

'Although he failed to retrieve the hoard, having had to flee the oasis for fear of his life, Hornemann retained a single parchment which he sent back to the University at Göttingen, in Lower Saxony. The University being one of the very few where Oriental languages were being studied at the time. He also included a map.'

Meyer produced a photostat of a sketch of the oasis. He also handed Arturo a photograph of the parchment. 'We want you to find this hoard. It is buried within sight of the Temple of Amun, as you can see on this chart.'

Chapter 16

I was shocked to see the parchment was almost identical to the one I had in my notebook. The script was indistinguishable. At first, I was reluctant to work for the Germans, but the Standartenführer made it quite obvious what would happen to me if I chose not to cooperate. It became clear to me that things might not go well. So I put my parchment in an envelope and intended to keep it safe by sending it to Marietta's place in Rome with the military post. I even got as far as the quartermaster's office.

But then the British attacked in the north. That night, lights flickered wildly on the horizon. Flashes and a continuous rumble disturbed the desert sky. Later on, I realised that with them, any hope of seeing Marietta soon, ended. The 136th Giovani Fascisti division pulled out and insisted I join them. Long columns of trucks left the oasis and headed west. The young soldiers of the brigade called out to me to leave, but I hesitated until my nerve cracked and I clambered aboard one of the last vehicles.

Then we began a long arduous journey across the desert. The whole line had collapsed after the battle at El Alamein. Finally, the division descended out of the foothills and reached the coastal town of Mersa Brega in Libya. It was December 1942. The Afrika Korps was in full retreat and the roads were clogged with vehicles of every description.

I left the young fascist unit sometime in February 1943 and tried to get to Tunis. I never made it. I was picked up on the coastal road by a British patrol. What possessions I had were taken and checked. The envelope with the parchment was stolen from me by a young grinning English boy. I pleaded with him not to take it, but he just pushed me to the sand and laughed. Although almost as an afterthought, he flung my journal back at me. Later, I was interned with other Italian civilians and forced to do menial work for the British. Finally, I was shipped to England.

I was released in 1945, but I had no money and no way of returning to Egypt. The day I was freed, I had every intention of trying to find your mother. Every day had been a torment of guilt and despair, not knowing what had happened to her. But how was I to get back to her? I was three thousand miles away.

By chance, in Brindisi, I met a girl from the Italian community of Cairo. The British had put me on a ship heading towards the Mediterranean and I had disembarked in southern Italy. She told me that your mother had left Egypt. Marietta had remained in the city for most of the war with the other Italian women but had vanished when the war ended. The girl thought she had returned to Rome.

I visited Marietta's family's house near the Termini station but it had gone, destroyed in an air raid. Eventually, I went back to work at the Institute. I was there ten years later when she walked into my office with you by her side. I dropped the teapot I had been holding. This is your daughter, she told me. I tried to explain, but it came out all wrong. Too much time had passed, and she didn't believe my story. Why did I desert her? Why hadn't I sent her a letter? I was in despair — maybe even more than if she hadn't come to see me in the first place.

Now I am too old, but I would very much like your mother to forgive me, to believe in me — just once more before I go — to relive that night amongst the jasmine and the lotus.

Chapter 17

Rome, Italy, present day

The silence lifted and sounds from the street below broke through their reverie. Anna murmured, 'That's so sad. Arturo and Marietta. A love never to be.' Michael just slowly shook his head. Anna rubbed her arms as if the temperature had just fallen. 'So that's it,' she whispered. 'The origin of the papyrus.'

'It seems so. It came from the oasis of Siwa. Part of some larger collection.'

'Wow.'

'What do we do now?' Michael looked around. The white-haired lady still hadn't returned. Picking up the book, he led Anna through the glass door. Only the young boy was there, slouching on a sofa in front of a television. 'Madame Eva?' Michael enquired.

The boy looked up impatiently and pointed upwards. 'Sleeping. You go now.'

Michael made to put the book down, but Anna grabbed his arm and shook her head once. She then pushed him towards the door. 'Thank you,' she murmured to the now indifferent boy and Michael followed her down the stairs and out into the quiet street. 'Before you say anything, we will return it when we have finished.' Anna's expression was quite firm.

'A loan then?'

'Yes. Agreed.'

Leaving the tall yellow terraced house, they headed towards the metro and took the line to the Piazza Bologna. They had researched this beforehand and there were many small pensioni in the area. It was also right next to the Sapienza University.

Anna and Michael found a suitable place a stone's throw away from the Piazza and after settling into their room, they walked to the nearest bookshop. It was rundown and filled with mostly second-hand books, many of them were textbooks written in Italian. The middle-aged proprietor watched them suspiciously as they wandered around the shelves. Anna finally found a tattered Baedeker's guide to Egypt in English that was only two years out of date.

The travel guide described Siwa as the most westerly of all the oases in Egypt. Pretty much the last habitable place before you reached

Libya. It was a mere thirty miles from the border. With the deteriorating situation in Libya, security was tight, but it was still possible to travel there, as long as they had a permit, available in Cairo or Alexandria.

Back at the Pensione Bari, Michael collapsed on one of the two single beds. They weren't paying much, so the sheets were thin and the pillows hard. 'What a day,' he commented. There was no reply from Anna, so he opened his eyes and found her standing over him. 'Everything okay?'

'Yes. Michael.' She sat down next to him, leant over and gently placed her lips over his. The lightest of touches, and yet the effect was exhilarating. A groan escaped from Michael's lips.

'Did you just groan?' Anna moved backwards and stared at him.

'No!' He sat up quickly, almost knocking their heads together.

'I'm sure it was.'

'No. It was … an unconscious sigh, I think.'

'A sigh. Mmm. Well, that's okay then,' she quipped lightly and pushed him back down on to the bed.

Sometime during the night, Michael woke — his mind unusually disturbed and try as he might he couldn't get back to sleep. Anna's breathing was soft and even. Making as little noise as he could, Michael rolled out of bed and sat at the small table next to the window. A diffuse glow on the horizon was the only hint of dawn.

He switched on a small lamp and angled it so it wouldn't disturb the girl and took out the archaeologist's notebook. Most entries had some form of a date near the top of the page. They ranged from 1941 through to 1943. The first few dozen pages were various descriptions of the excavation near Lake Qarun, in the Faiyum basin. Halfway through, the entries became more haphazard … brief sketches and scribbled notes. Then there was a page with Siwa circled in red at the top.

Here the Italian archaeologist had drawn a plan of the Siwan's land. Contour lines, boundaries and physical structures like irrigation ditches and rocks were all noted — then at the very bottom, a cryptic series of shapes and numbers.

'What you doing up?' Anna's voice was thick with slumber.

'Couldn't sleep. Looking at the journal.'

She slipped out from under the sheets, came over and put her arm over Michael's shoulder. Her skin smelt very slightly of lemons.

Anna regarded the sketch sceptically. 'How big is the oasis?' she questioned.

He referred back to the travel book. 'Fifty miles by twelve.'

'I don't think we are going to find this,' she pointed to the map. 'In all of that.' Her finger dropped to the bottom of the page. 'These shapes don't make any sense either.'

Michael too had already contemplated the simple row of angular shapes — a single rectangle with a zero above it, a space then a group of three trapezium shapes with the number 23 above them, a much larger space followed by a single triangle and the number 125. And finally, the last shape with 164.

Michael slumped down, his elbows on the table, head in his hands. 'Oh, I don't know! We don't seem to be getting a break here.' The leather backed journal contained all the clues they had. He couldn't see a way forward. Rifling through the pages, he came across the passage about Ulrich Meyer. Why did the archaeologist record the meeting in so much detail? It seemed strange. Michael re-read the words. It then jumped out at him.

'Anna. What if this guy Hornemann found the original stash of documents? Look at the date. 1798.'

'What's so significant about that?'

'No one could decipher any Egyptian languages properly until after 1800 and something. Champollion and all that.'

'Whoa. You've lost me, Michael.'

'Egyptian wasn't properly deciphered until after 1822. I'm sure you have heard of the Rosetta stone?'

'Kind of.'

'It's a black granite stele. A stone tablet on which a proclamation had been inscribed in three different languages: Hieroglyphics, Greek and Demotic. The stone had been cut in a quarry near Aswan in Upper Egypt, probably around 200BC. On it was carved a decree from the newly crowned pharaoh, Ptolemy the Fifth. The Greek was used by the Frenchman, Champollion and the English physician, Young, to figure out how the Hieroglyphics and Demotic script were used and Egyptian could be translated.'

'So?'

'Hornemann couldn't have known what any of the papyri were. They would have been … as you so rightly said before, gibberish to him.'

'Right.'

'He probably found them, hid them in a stone jar, meaning to come and dig it up later. Unfortunately, he was forced to flee before he could reclaim it.'

'Mmm.'

'And he drew a chart of where he buried it.'

Anna picked up the journal and ran her finger along the passage. She read it aloud as she went, 'Hornemann retained a single parchment which he sent back to the University at Göttingen, in Lower Saxony. He also included a map. Meyer produced a photostat of a sketch of the oasis.' She paused and questioned Michael, 'Photostat. What's that?'

'An early version of a photocopy, I think.'

'So, they didn't have the original. It could still be there in Göttingen.'

Chapter 18

Göttingen, Germany, present day

Above, the stone-washed clouds were darkening with the threat of rain and the onset of dusk. The grey buildings of the university faded into the brooding sky — almost all of the windows were dark, now that it was the end of the day. Across the paved square was the library of the University of Göttingen, a sleek metal and glass structure, lit from within by strip lights that offered some comfort in the chilly evening.

Michael and Anna's long train journey up from Rome was best forgotten about. Changes at Verona and Stuttgart were a blur of dashes between platforms. The one highlight for Michael had been that Anna had fallen asleep, nuzzled up against him for most of the trip through Germany. Now they strode up the steps and entered through a revolving door. In front of them was a modern reception desk behind which sleek white columns and racks of bookshelves receded into the distance.

'Hallo. Darf ich dir helfen?' inquired the young woman behind the counter.

'Ja…' Michael began, but a sharp dig in his ribs from Anna stopped him. 'Sorry. Do you speak English?'

'Yes. What can I do for you?' the receptionist replied with a crisp yet bright accent.

'We are looking for any material that is connected with Fredrich Hornemann. A German explorer of North Africa.'

'I am not familiar with this name.'

'He was in Egypt in 1798.'

'Oh, that is a long time ago,' the receptionist turned to a computer terminal.

'Probably some form of travelogue?' Michael offered.

She stopped typing and looked up from the screen. 'I fear you are in the wrong place. Books and manuscripts from 1700 to 1900 are housed in the old building.' The girl took a pamphlet from a stack on the counter, turned it over and circled a building on the map. 'But the archives there are restricted. They are not open to the public.' The girl looked apologetic.

After making their way to the centre of the town, Anna and Michael searched for a guesthouse and booked in for the night. The sky had blackened and an avalanche of rain pounded the pavement.

'We need some sort of reference to get in,' Anna stated once they had closed the guestroom door.

'Frank. He knows all sorts of people in the University back home.'

'Maybe you should call him then.'

Michael picked up the telephone on the bedside table and dialled for an outside line. 'It's five here, so he should still be at the Registry.'

The phone rang several times and then it was answered abruptly. 'OADR. How can I help you?'

'Frank. It's Michael.'

There was a short pause, and then Frank's voice boomed cheerfully, 'Michael, my boy. Still living it up in America?'

'No. No. I am on my way home. But I called for some help.'

'What is it, lad?' More concern in his words now.

'I'm actually in Germany.'

'Germany!' Frank's speech increased in pitch.

'Yes. It's a long story and I will tell you everything soon. But right now, I need to ask you if you can get me into the Restricted Archives at the University of Göttingen's Library.'

'What are you doing there Michael?'

'As I said, I will tell you, but first I need that access. Do you know anyone there?'

'Well, not specifically. But I do know the Head of the Staatsbibliothek. She might be able to do something.'

'Could you get her to vouch for me?'

'Let me call her now. Where can I reach you?'

Michael wiped a stain off the telephone and read off the number at the guesthouse.

An hour passed painfully slowly, as they waited to hear back from Frank. Anna curled up on an armchair and Michael paced incessantly around the room. Finally, the room phone rang.

'Well, she has arranged you to see the Senior Archivist at 11am tomorrow. Are you going to let me know what you're up to?'

'Soon,' Michael promised and put down the phone. 'We're in. 11 o'clock.'

Chapter 19

Oxford, England, present day

Wind rattled the window panes of the old wooden hut. Brief gusts sounded out a staccato of Morse code-like knocks. But the lone figure, hunched over the desk, barely moved as he put down the receiver.

Frank eyed the ledger in front of him. The figures were bad. Costs were rising and grants drying up. The Registry building was on its last legs. In a world obsessed with technology and economic growth, no one was funding archaeology anymore, let alone papyrology. Student numbers had been dropping precipitously and departments were closing all across the country. The formation of the Registry had been his idea, but it was only loosely associated with one of the colleges. The project, which he had devoted his life to, was struggling. He briefly deliberated for a few moments before picking up the receiver once more. Without any preamble, he stated, 'They're at the University of Göttingen. The Rare Archives Building. They have an appointment at 11am tomorrow. Can Alex and Gethan make it there?'

The voice on the other end replied, 'I don't see why not? They've been kicking their heels in London these past few days. They can get an evening flight to Frankfurt, pick up a car and be in Saxony before morning.' Smith's tone was calm and reassuring.

'Michael and the girl must know something more. Otherwise, why go all the way to Germany? There's something else we're not getting.'

'Mmm. You're probably right. They should have hit a dead end. You have done the right thing, Frank. Well done.'

As Frank put down the handset, he muttered, 'God only knows, I hope so.'

Chapter 20

Göttingen, Germany, present day

The Rare Archives were housed in the old library, part of the original university buildings set up in 1734. It had been substantially restored and its pale lemon walls and huge carved entrance were a throwback to grander times.

Anna and Michael walked up the wide stone steps a few minutes before their appointment. With characteristic Germanic efficiency, they were welcomed at the door by a middle-aged woman with stern features and hair that was already turning grey. After a brief introduction, Michael informed her of their interest.

'Hornemann. Fredrich Hornemann. 1798 you say?'

'Yes. Where do you think we should start?'

'Mmm. Let's go to the database first.' Instead of going to a filing cabinet, as he had expected, the Senior Archivist went to a computer and started typing in the keywords. 'We have completely digitised our record system and are in the process of making all our books available in digital format.'

She scanned the screen. 'Now let me see. Ah, yes. Here we have some entries. Fredrich Hornemann. He was born in 1772, in a town just north of here. A German explorer attached to the African Society. He was a student of this university where he studied Arabic. Interesting. He travelled through Egypt and across the desert to Southern Libya. He died in Africa in 1819. '

There was a delay as she read through some of the information. 'I have no specific books penned by him though, here at this library.'

'No journals?'

'No. Nothing. But I do see that there exists a translation of his journal by a Major Rennell. Travels from Cairo to Mourzouk in 1797. We don't have a copy of that, but you can find a copy from the New York Public Library online.' She looked up at Michael expectantly. He thought for a moment but couldn't come up with anything to ask her.

Anna moved closer to the computer and pointed out the words, African Society. 'What's that?'

The librarian tapped out a few commands and then spoke, 'It was an organisation based in London. Interestingly, we do have a quite a few legacy documents for this association. A society for promoting the exploration of Inner Africa,' she recited from the screen. 'There are some reports and a fair bit of correspondence.' She clicked on a few entries and looked at them ruefully. 'They are not digitised. You will have to go through them by hand, I'm afraid.'

While they waited for the material to be collected from the shelves, Michael asked the librarian if she had heard of the Ahnenerbe Institute. It had been mentioned in the Italian archaeologist's journal and he thought it might be important — maybe another lead to investigate.

The grey-haired lady looked at him over her glasses. 'It was the Nazi pseudo-archaeology unit, set up just before the war. They tried to substantiate the claim that Germany was the cradle of civilisation — to justify its status as a racially superior race. They reinterpreted the past, even suggesting that the ancient Greeks were Germanic.'

She gave them an exasperated look. 'Most of the modern fascination with the Nazi occult is salacious fiction. But it was true that they sent out investigators to various places around the globe. To dig up artifacts that supported their perverted view of the world.'

Soon an assistant brought them two much worn books and a box file. 'If you would like to go to the reading room at the end of the corridor, you will not be disturbed.' She indicated for them to follow her. 'Unfortunately, you cannot take your bags. Maybe you can leave them here on this table.'

They dumped their stuff and followed her to the back of the library. Before parting, the assistant offered, 'Shall I see if there is anything else we can find?' Anna nodded as she accepted the books from her.

Chapter 21

Göttingen, Germany, present day

The two large volumes were in poor shape and as expected carried the distinctive sickly odour of old books. Michael took one and Anna the other, then they patiently worked their way through them. But there was nothing about Hornemann and almost no mention of Egypt. Turning to the box file, Michael started to lift out each piece and examine it. Much of it was musty and heavily discoloured, but near the back he was finally rewarded. He saw the words —

Oase Siwah, Agypten, 1798

It was written on a thin pamphlet of no more than six pages, held together very loosely between ox-hide covers. He gingerly flicked through the sheets.

Handwritten on the first page, in German, was an entry that Michael slowly read out to Anna, translating as he went, *"An account of the discoveries made at the oasis of Siwa."* He turned to her and grinned. She motioned for him to carry on. Michael turned over the page and started to translate.

"I feel sick with fear. The tightness in my stomach hasn't left me since Baruasch. For fifteen days, I have walked among men who would cut my throat if they knew who I was. This evening, we crested a long ridge and there below us was a valley that stretched to the horizon, filled with trees, the only habitable place in this vast wasteland.

As the long line of men and animals climbed down towards the trees, here and there, I could see several lights coming from low buildings. A small settlement gathered at the base of a low hill. Then, just as the sun cleared the clouds and before it dipped below the horizon, light picked out the shape of massive stones lost among the date palms.

After a brief exchange with one of the pilgrims, my interpreter relayed the information. They were ruins built by the infidels who had inhabited the oasis a long time ago.

A large group of natives had by this time gathered by the roadside. Attracted by the heavily laden camels, they had abandoned their work in the fields. Clearly our fairer skin was of some concern to them and several pointed at us with obvious dislike.

Eventually they pointed out a plain to the west where we could make camp. The main town, if you could call *it that, was built around the base of a stony hill, the houses small and packed closely together."*

Michael stopped for a while and allowed his eyes to refocus. Translating it was very intense. The German was a little antiquated.

'Michael. Just summarize it. Give me the main points,' Anna chided him.

'Alright.' He scanned the next few paragraphs. 'Okay. He says something about the people. Natives challenge him. He defends himself saying he is a Turk. A pilgrim vouches for him. He investigates the oasis. He travels several miles to check on the local claims of catacombs, salt springs and the ruins of the Ammonites. He is told the ruins contain gold buried under the walls.'

Michael stopped and turned over another page. 'It is here he enters an inner sepulchre and digging down uncovers a … Steingutbehälter … I think that means a stone or earthenware jar. He covers it and returns that night to dig it up with his servant. They move it but are disturbed and leave it only half buried. Some documents are taken to make copies. But every time he approaches the ruins he is accompanied by natives and he cannot investigate any more. He is challenged that he must be an infidel again. Locals have the impression that the ruins are of Christian origin. The documents have writing he cannot understand. He is sending it to the university, to the department of Oriental Studies for translation.' The last page was torn at the bottom and the end of the text was missing.

'That's all?' Anna asked.

'Yes. If there was any more, then it must be elsewhere. Is there any sign of the papyrus he sent back to the university?'

Anna picked up the stack of documents from the file and slowly but surely went through them again. 'No. Nothing.'

Michael pointed to the computer at the back of the room, 'Do you think we should check his journal? I'm sure we can access the online copy from here. The translation by Rennell.'

Anna sat down at the keyboard and started typing. Within a few minutes, a scan of the book appeared on the screen. It was prefaced by a section detailing the preparations and reasons for the expedition. Next came several chapters, each one corresponding to various sections of the journey. There were two that focused on the time at Siwa.

They quickly read through these accounts. It was quite fascinating, but it didn't add anything more to what they already knew, although Michael noticed that Hornemann made no mention of finding any documents in the ruins.

Michael took up the small booklet and carefully examined each page. Finally, he came to the end of the pamphlet. He was about to pop it back into the box file when he noticed a very small crease on the last page. At the back, a sheet of slightly darker parchment was inserted. It looked like it was the endpaper, the paper glued to the cover, but in fact, Michael realised, it was just stuck there with age. Carefully, he prised it away and unfolded it.

The map was cleverly drawn on a single sheet of thin and pliable vellum, folded just once. The edges were a deep golden colour but most of the map was pale and quite readable. Dark ink lines traced out an extensive portion of the oasis with intricate little drawings of the major important features: the edge of a lake, a circular pool, the square-enclosed walls of a temple. Minuscule inscriptions in German littered the chart and near the top of the map there was, quite remarkably, a cross marked. But it was all out of proportion, almost like a child's drawing.

Anna and Michael slowly made their way back to the front desk. Michael carefully put the box file down and asked the librarian at the counter if they could copy some of the documents.

'Yes. That is possible.' She pointed to a grey slab of a machine pushed up into the corner. 'Although there is a slight charge.'

'I've got some small change in my backpack.' Michael looked over to where he had left it. His canvas bag wasn't there. He searched the floor and under the table. It was gone.

'What's the matter?' Anna inquired.

'My bag? It's not here. Has someone else been here?'

The librarian looked confused. 'The other people? The Americans? They are not with you?'

'What Americans?' Anna questioned, looking around the library. But they both could see that no one else was there.

Chapter 22

Oxfordshire, England, present day

The large Georgian manor house was situated at the end of a wide sweeping driveway and nestled between manicured lawns and a small lake. Frank had been shown into a large reception room by a young lady. This was the first time he had been invited down to the thin man's residence. Normally they met in a quiet or out-of-the-way place, typically the Ashmolean Museum or one of Oxford's many college gardens. Actually, Frank rather enjoyed the skulduggery of it all — to him it was a piece of harmless theatre.

The room was laid out with numerous tables and cabinets. As he waited for his benefactor to appear, he examined some of the items on display. There were some Hebrew scrolls that looked Kabbalistic, Judean stone tablets and many silver coins: Tyrian shekels, Athenian drachmas and staters from Antioch.

There was also a parchment codex of the Book of Enoch locked away in a glass case, yellow with age and garishly illustrated. This was one of the foremost Lost Books of the Bible. Texts referred to in the Old and New Testaments but never discovered. It had been re-found in the middle of Abyssinia of all places. The Book of Enoch had been mentioned in the canonical Book of Jude, but all traces of it had been ruthlessly excised by the Jewish Sanhedrin in 90AD, not a single Aramaic or Greek copy had been left. However, they forgot about the conversion of Ethiopian travellers who had taken their texts with them far beyond the reach of the Pharisees. It was in Abyssinia that the Scottish explorer James Bruce had found a copy of it written in the Ethiopian language of Ge'ez. The work was otherworldly — it involved the fall of the Angels and an account of Enoch as he travelled through heaven.

Surveying the whole room, Frank began to get a much clearer idea of the true passion behind Mr Smith's motives.

'Frank.' The assertion made him jump. He spun around. The thin man had seemingly appeared out of nowhere.

'This is quite … quite a collection,' Frank stammered.

'Yes. But it is much more than a collection. It is evidence.'

'Of what?'

'A great truth. Hidden mysteries and a repressed history.' He held up a finger. 'But finding it? That is the hard part.'

Smith passed a picture to Frank. 'I pushed Alex to give us a photograph of the papyrus he stole. We are going to have to deal with him at some point. He's a bit strong-headed, but I think he'll come around.'

Frank looked at the facsimile of the old fragment. It was the first time he'd had a chance to really study the document. 'Well, there appears to be a dozen lines of text. Running left to right. Some of it appears missing from the top and bottom. Definitely very old Coptic. Egyptian. It seems it was hurriedly written. See here, the scribe has run several letters together. A very cursive hand.'

'What's this?' Smith pointed to the last two lines.

'This is what intrigued Michael. It is scratched out in rather coarse Aramaic. And as usual it is written from right to left. This part is a name. Shim-on. Then Kan-anai. Zealot.'

'What do we really know about Simon the Zealot?' asked Smith.

'Almost nothing,' confessed Frank. 'A single mention of his name in each book and then he might as well have disappeared. Though I believe there is a Muslim tradition that he journeyed amongst the Berbers of North Africa. Some other medieval traditions have him as a companion of Judas Thaddeus, accompanying him on missions to Persia.'

'Judas and Simon. Both disciples. Isn't there some possibility that they were half-brothers?'

'Maybe, but many names were used interchangeably and a case for either situation can be made. But interestingly, Judas Thaddeus was sometimes called Judas the Zealot.'

'What about the rest?'

'Texts written in this pre-Coptic form are quite rare. The few that have survived are pagan magical spells. Nothing Christian.' Frank studied the image once more. 'It was used to prevent the mispronunciation of the incantation.'

'But why wouldn't it be written in plain Greek? Surely that was the more common language at the time?'

'To mask its meaning. To keep it secret. Greek was used precisely because it could be understood by many and whatever was written down could be read out to others.'

The thin man looked pensive and then beamed at Frank. 'But the age of the document intrigues me. The closer you get to the original source, surely the more accurate the words must be ... less time to corrupt the real truth?'

A sound trilled in the quietness. Smith reached inside his jacket and lifted a mobile phone from deep inside his pocket.

'Yes?' He frowned. 'Wait a minute.' He touched the screen and immediately the voice of Alex sounded from the speakerphone.

'I'm sitting inside Frankfurt airport terminal. Looks like they're going to take a flight to Cairo.'

The thin man's eyes widened. 'Rewind, Alex.'

'Yeah, right. Forgot you're not up to speed.'

'From the beginning. What did you find?'

'Yesterday, they spent the day at the library. I overheard the staff looking for something about North Africa.'

'Nothing more? They didn't see you.'

'No. But I got the boy's bag and there ain't nothing in it.'

Frank swore under his breath but the thin man held up his finger. 'Alex. Don't do anything to spook them.' Frank turned his back and moved to the window.

'Don't worry old man. I got this. This morning they got a bus to Frankfurt airport. Gethan's got a seat on the same flight. He'll follow them when they land. I'm catching a slightly later flight. I want to pick up some gear from a friend of mine.'

Smith had wandered several feet away from Frank and now he lowered his voice and said, 'Okay. I'm going to send you details of a contact in Cairo. He is someone I've used before. He'll act as your driver and guide.'

'I think we can manage,' Alex responded indignantly.

'No. Seriously, you can't. Not there. He is ex-Mabahith Amn el-Dawla.'

'What's that?'

'The Paramilitary Police.'

'Shit.'

'Just keep a low profile.'

'You sure these international roaming cards will work anywhere?'

'Yes. So keep in contact.'

Chapter 23

Cairo, Egypt, present day

The grey city sprawled across the landscape.
Hemmed in by the desert plateau to the west, it
straddled both sides of the Nile. Northwards it
blossomed into the fertile, lush green delta, but
to the south it became pinched by the narrow
river valley. Cairo was the largest city in Africa
and home to twenty million people.

The decision to fly there was taken after Anna
had spent two hours analysing the pros and cons
of seeing the search through to the end — or at
least as far as it was possible to go. 'I think it
really just hinges on how safe it is to move
around Egypt and get to Siwa by ourselves.'

'Bearing in mind, I don't have any access to
money,' Michael added. When his bag had been
stolen, he had lost his wallet with most of his
cash and all of his bank cards. Luckily, he still
had his passport, which he had kept in his inside
jacket pocket.

'I've got enough to cover us for now,' Anna
reassured.

She continued, 'I took the initiative to contact an Irish lady who has lived there for the last ten years. Found her name on the internet. She runs a small tour company and sounds like she knows her stuff.'

'What did she say?'

'The situation has certainly stabilized over the past four years. She recommended the usual: don't go walking down dark streets, stick to the main tourist areas and so on. But she felt it was as safe as any country can be.'

'Anything specific about Siwa?'

'She said, although it's near the Libyan border, the security is pretty relaxed. Not like in Upper Egypt. There, the police escort tourist groups as a standard precaution.'

Travelling to the city centre in a battered mustard-yellow taxi was a nightmare. The noise and heat were beyond anything Michael had experienced before. The cacophony from car horns was continuous. Their guidebook had advised them not to bother with the bus — typically overcrowded and slow. They were heading to the Garden Hostel, apparently in walking distance to Tahrir Square, the de facto centre of the city.

Cars and taxis filled the roads, swerving in and out of lanes. Traffic lurched from one jam to the next but eventually they arrived at the hostel, paid the driver and entered the modern yet dilapidated looking establishment. A loud screech made Michael look around, but it was just some altercation between a silver-grey SUV and a donkey cart.

The polite receptionist slowly processed their information and after completing several forms, they were escorted by an elderly man in a blue galabiya to their room.

'Let's get some rest and then figure out what to do next,' Anna said.

Later that evening, they wandered along the wide streets of the Sharia Talaat Harb. The buildings reminded Michael of a slightly rundown Parisian quarter. Anna had wrapped her hair up and tucked into a beanie. They both wore jeans and jackets. Even so, they still got several stares from passing people.

'Getting to Siwa isn't as difficult as it used to be, apparently. No police or military authorisation is required. I asked at the front desk and there are basically three ways of getting there.'

'Which are?' Anna asked.

'There's a bus that goes there direct. Takes twelve hours and leaves late at night. The second is to hire a car and driver who will take us there.'

'Too expensive?'

'Probably,' confirmed Michael.

'Then there's a train to Alexandria and Mersa Matruh, followed by a bus to the oasis.'

'That sounds too roundabout. And slower.'

'Okay, then we'll get the evening bus.'

'Can we do it tomorrow? I'm bushed.'

'Oh yes. I would like to take you to the Coptic Museum before we leave.'

'Why?'

'There is someone there I would like you to meet.'

The museum was on the south side of the city, close to the river and set within the compound of an old Roman fortress. In the morning, they took the Metro line running towards Helwan and got off at Mar Girgis, just opposite the museum. The compound's pitted ochre limestone walls were a stark contrast to the modern marbled slabs that clad the station. Passing the domed structure of the monastery of Saint George, they entered through the main gate. A pair of swallows flitted amongst the columns and palm trees as they made their way across the courtyard.

After showing their passports to the security guards, they entered the foyer and paid for two tickets. Several glass cabinets held various icons and other antiquities, and above them soared an ornate carved wooden ceiling.

'I think it should be this way,' Michael directed Anna down a side corridor. 'We are going to where they keep some of the oldest artifacts. In the Department of Manuscripts.'

Michael knocked on a wooden door and waited for an answer. It opened after a minute and a short lady in a long dress stood before them. With a puzzled look, she enquired, 'Can I help?'

'Hello, Madame Falisha. It is Michael. Michael from the OADR.'

'Michael! Is it really you?'

'Yes. And I was in Cairo and thought I would put a face to my name.' He turned to a surprised Anna and explained, 'We have corresponded over the last year. Many times. Madame Falisha is a world-renowned expert on the Coptic language.'

'Michael, you make me blush.' She stepped aside and invited them into the Department's office. 'How is Frank?'

'Oh, he's good.'

'Not with you?'

'No. It's just us. This is my friend Anna.'

Falisha eyed Anna with obvious suspicion, clearly not certain how to acknowledge her. 'Anna is a carbon dating expert with the University of Arizona. She's worked on some of the Dead Sea Scrolls,' he quickly added.

'Oh, that's fascinating.' The curator visibly relaxed.

They talked for a few minutes before Michael brought up the main purpose of their visit. 'I was wondering if I could show Anna the type of document you process here. Perhaps the Schmidt Papyrus?'

'How did you know we have that?' The woman was a little surprised.

'Frank said you mentioned it once to him. During a late night at some conference. He wasn't entirely sure whether it was just a slip of the tongue.'

Carl Schmidt was a German academic who travelled widely throughout Egypt purchasing archaic manuscripts for German universities. He was an eminent coptologist. The Schmidt Papyrus, as it became known, had been found by him in 1937 shortly before his death. However, it was missing from his final possessions. Its existence was only known because of a photograph he had passed to a colleague.

She sighed and signalled us to follow her. 'We have it in a locked cabinet over here. Did you know Schmidt passed away here in Cairo? He entrusted it to the Museum in 1938 with some restrictions. But just a quick look. You really should have written beforehand.'

Michael promised and apologised once more, but the lady was incredibly proud of her collection and promptly removed the glass-encased papyrus from a showcase.

'I've been telling Anna how the Coptic language replaced Ancient Egyptian Demotic.'

Madame Falisha looked at the document with a cool detachment. 'Demotic was a fiendishly difficult script. There were no vowels. By the first century, how the language was spoken had become quite different to how it was written. I think later scribes forgot how to fill in the spaces and were forced to write Egyptian with Greek characters.'

Michael took out his notebook. 'What about a Proto-Coptic cursive script using these glyphs?' he enquired, pointing to some of the characters he had transcribed from the papyrus fragment so many days before in Oxford.

'It would be old. There are so few examples of Old Coptic left. It is incredibly rare. Since most were spells invoking Egyptian gods, they were ruthlessly destroyed over the years.' She paused and looked at Anna. 'I don't know if Michael has explained this to you, but the usual Coptic alphabet consists of twenty-four characters taken from the Greek alphabet and seven glyphs borrowed from Demotic. They were needed to represent sounds in Egyptian not available in Greek. So, a Coptic text looks a bit like a Greek one, but it bears no relation to the vocabulary, grammar or syntax of the Greek language. What Michael is indicating are Demotic glyphs that aren't part of the standard seven. They could represent alternative ways of pronunciation or even a personal code for that particular scribe.'

Madam Falisha lifted up the glass frame and proceeded to put it back into the storage cabinet. 'This isn't even a Christian text. It is in fact a prayer. A plea for help from a pagan god. A woman who wants a man to do the right thing.'

'Sounds like nothing's changed,' quipped Anna.

Madame Falisha laughed. 'Yes, dear. History is full of women seeking justice from the men who have done them wrong.'

Chapter 24

Cairo, Egypt, present day

Before they left the museum, Anna strolled into the little gift shop just off the main entrance. The space was obviously a new addition to the building, and it was still in the process of being finished, with plastic sheeting and workmen's tools piled in one of the corners. The few completed cabinets were full of vaguely antique looking objects and there were racks of postcards and shelves of guide books. A few other tourists were milling about the shop, including a small group of Japanese and a red-headed guy checking out souvenirs in the corner.

Anna spent several minutes perusing the bookcase, then reached up and took down a thin paperback. Bringing it over to Michael, she pointed to the cover. 'Let's get this. The Oasis of Siwa by Ahmed Fakry,' she said. Michael briefly flicked through the pages before he bobbed his head in agreement.

They wandered out into the courtyard and headed towards the metro station. Behind them, the other tourists followed them out. Michael stopped at a small cart on the roadside. A teenage boy was selling sugared chickpeas in cones of rolled up newspaper. Michael quickly conversed with him and passed him some coins in exchange for two packets.

Anna reached out to take one. 'How come you know so much Arabic?'

'I pick up little bits of lots of languages. As you know, I can speak a little German. A bit of Italian and even some English.' Anna rolled her eyes at him over that one. 'But Arabic I learned on the one time I accompanied my father on a dig in Jordan. He left me alone for much of the day, so I spent it talking to some of the workmen. They taught me the basics.'

Before they left to catch the bus to Siwa, Michael insisted they take a detour. It didn't take long, and they were soon wandering past tall jacarandas and soaring palms. The place was a bit shabby, but it had a somewhat Bohemian air — no doubt due to the black and silver horse-drawn carriages that lined the road. Small family groups dressed in their finest gathered nearby, waiting to take rides around the quiet neighbourhood.

'What is this place?' Anna inquired.

'These are the Gardens of Gezira,' Michael replied. They had crossed over onto the island that divided the banks of the Nile, west of Tahrir Square.

Anna's initial bewilderment turned to understanding. 'Marietta and Arturo!'

'Yes. Where they first fell in love. At least it could be the place, don't you think?'

They strolled hand-in-hand under an ancient ficus tree — its dangling roots hanging like chains that sliced the sunlight. The ground nearby was scrappy and the plants forlorn but set amongst the concrete and brick that suffocated the city, it was a haven of calm.

At seven o'clock that evening, they walked into the modern Gateway Plaza which had replaced the old Turgoman Bus Station, just north of the city centre. A security officer indicated that they should pass their bags through a scanner and afterwards they headed to a set of ticket counters on the left. The whole place was almost deserted.

Anna suddenly pulled up sharply. 'Wait,' she stated. 'We must get some water for the journey.' She spun around and walked back the way they had come, her eyes scanning to locate a suitable shop. Michael turned and rushed to catch up and promptly bumped straight into her. She had stopped again.

Anna was staring at a man maybe twenty feet away — a European or American, tall and bearded, wearing a blue cotton jacket and jeans. He dropped his chin, trying to hide his face, and hurried towards the main entrance.

'Who was that?' Michael asked.

Anna looked flummoxed. 'It can't be.'

'Can't be who?'

'The visiting lecturer in Tucson. The one who came into the lab.'

'You're sure?'

'Yes, Michael. I'm sure.'

'What's he doing here?'

'It's obvious. He's following us.' Anna strode towards the entrance. 'And I'm going to ask him why.'

By the time Michael caught up with her, she was already outside the Station. Anna stood on the edge of the pavement. Further down the road, a grey SUV sulked by the kerbside. The denim-clad man opened the passenger's door and climbed in. Next to him was a swarthy, grim-

146

faced person in a leather coat. Anna drew out her phone and held it up to take a photograph. Suddenly, the car erupted out of the shadows and sped towards her.

Michael reached out, grabbed Anna's arm and pulled her behind him. The SUV, its headlights flashing across the building in front of them, screeched to a halt and Michael heard the doors open. But he never looked back. 'Come on,' he cried out to her.

They ran across the road. Michael saw the lights of a taxi. He waved his arms for it to stop. It pulled up, the side window down. A toothless driver in a white fez grinned at them. 'Fein?' the old man croaked.

Michael pushed Anna inside and slammed the door. 'Imshi,' he barked. The driver struggled to put the car into gear — racking the gearstick several times before the car lurched forward. 'The river. An-Nil.' It was all Michael could think of.

Behind them the SUV had backed up, swung around and was now charging towards them, its lights flooding the inside of the worn-out cab. It pulled wide to overtake. But just as it was about to get in front, it was forced to swerve back by oncoming cars. The most one-sided car chase in the history of the world, thought Michael — a clapped-out Fiat against a souped-up Toyota Land Cruiser. Oblivious to the pursuit, their fez wearing driver babbled away, gesturing enthusiastically with alternate hands.

Suddenly, the road ahead became a wall of red lights. They had run into one of Cairo's ubiquitous traffic jams. But their driver didn't let this stop him. Immediately the little Fiat taxi nudged its way through the milling throng, taking any advantage the driver could find. At one point, he had one set of wheels up on the pavement as it squeezed past a stalled truck. The car cantered crazily over, Anna pressed up against the door. Michael hoped to God that it wouldn't fly open by itself. Then they were through, cars ahead speeding up as they cleared the obstruction — a water buffalo in the middle of the road!

A few long breaths, then behind them, Michael glimpsed a streak of silver. 'Turn here,' he indicated wildly, and the driver yanked down on the steering wheel. They were thrown to the right, Anna ending up in the footwell. Peering through the rear window, Michael could see no sign of their pursuers. 'Mahaa! Good,' he praised the driver, who cracked a toothless smile at them.

The taxi was soon barrelling down a narrow lane, the rutted road lined with trash. Without warning, the driver switched off his headlights. Their world plunged into grey.

'What's he doing?' cried Anna.

'Frank said they do this all the time,' blurted Michael. The car sped down the street and swung onto a major road. Michael had no idea where they were going. The roads all looked the same. Then they bumped up onto a bridge and through the parapet he could see the Nile gleaming in the dark.

'They're coming,' Anna called. She had managed to get up and was looking behind them. Michael saw the silver Land Cruiser motoring fast down the outside lane, about four cars behind.

'Stop!' he shouted.

The old man fairly stood on the brakes and they had to brace themselves against the front seats. The SUV sailed past. Michael had a banknote out of his shirt pocket and waved it at the driver. 'This way.' Michael grabbed Anna's hand and pulled her from the car. 'Across the bridge.'

They dodged and skipped a few cars, and Michael leapt over the central dividing wall. Anna followed. The concrete barrier had weathered decades of abuse, it was chipped and cracked. As Anna rolled over the top, a protruding iron rod caught her side and dug into her abdomen. 'Fuck.' she cried out and collapsed onto the ground. Her bag spilled across the tarmac, scattering money, phone and documents. Without thinking, Michael leapt into the road, desperate to grab her things but only managed to reach her passport before being forced back by the oncoming cars.

Anna was bent almost double, and her eyes were squeezed shut. 'It's fucking painful.' The words said through clenched teeth.

'Can you move?'

'I think I can stand,' she nodded.

Suddenly, there was a horn blast — a taxi driver leaning out of his window and questioning with his hand.

'Yes. Come on. Let's get out of here.' Michael supported Anna and helped her into the taxi, which was a big improvement from the first one. 'To Tahrir square,' he commanded the driver.

Then to Anna he said, 'We have to get you to a doctor.'

'No. A pharmacy.'

'A clinic at least,' Michael insisted.

'It's not that serious. I just need to rest.'

Chapter 25

Cairo, Egypt, present day

Michael pulled out his hand phone and looked at the screen. 'Damn. There's no service.'

'Who do you want to call?'

'We need help. Money, as well. One of our embassies? Surely, they should be able to help us.'

'Where to call?'

'I'm thinking some sort of government office.' He hadn't noticed a single call box on the streets.

'A post office?' Anna muttered breathlessly.

Michael took out the folded tourist map he had picked up at the airport. 'Or telephone exchange.' He pointed to a phone symbol marked on one of the streets. 'This should do it.'

The brown plaster-covered building was several streets over from where the taxi had let them out. There was no sign of the grey Toyota. Michael supported Anna as they stumbled up to the main information desk. He asked the man behind the counter for the phone number of the British Consulate.

'It is very late. They are all closed.'

'What?'

'Yes, sir. All closed.' Michael looked at his watch and saw it was well past eight.

Anna sagged onto the floor. 'Who else?' she croaked.

Leaving her briefly, Michael walked over to a glass partition and asked if he could make a long-distance call. He wrote down the number and passed it to the young woman behind the counter.

'Over there. Cubicle three,' she motioned.

Michael squeezed into the small space. Anna took to a small chair outside. He waited for a few minutes, and then the telephone trilled. Picking it up, there was a brief moment where he could hear both the Egyptian operator and Frank's voice.

'Michael? Michael? Is that you?'

'Yes. Yes.'

'Are you okay, my boy?'

'Yes. Well … no. We are in a spot of trouble.'

'What was that? The line went dead just then.'

'A spot of trouble.'

'What is it?'

'We're being chased. Don't know who, but they are serious.'

'Chased? How can that be? Why are they after you?'

'I think it's the papyrus fragment. The Simon Zealot one.'

There was an abrupt silence and Michael thought the line had gone dead again. 'Frank?'

'Yes. Yes. I'm still here. You say the Simon Zealot papyrus? The one we … discarded?'

'Yes. But I kept it. There is something about it. Well … was.'

'What do you mean by was?'

'It's gone. It was destroyed in a fire.' Michael stopped for a moment. 'It was two thousand years old. Anna carbon dated it. Now it's gone.'

'I'm not sure I am following this. This is a lot to take in. It all seems out of character for you, Michael.'

'I know but you have to believe me.'

'Well, come home.'

'We can't. I think there are more.'

'More of what? More people chasing you?'

'No. More documents.'

'Like the papyrus?'

'Yes. We have good evidence that it's from one of the Egyptian oases.'

'Egypt?' Frank's tone was cautious, guarded. 'Are you there now?'

'Yes. In Cairo. But we don't have any money and Anna is hurt. Some men are after us.'

Frank went quiet for some time. 'I can't do anything for you. I'm too far away.' There was a crackling on the line and Frank's voice was distorted, then he repeated. 'But maybe your mother can.'

Chapter 26

Cairo, Egypt, present day

After paying for the call with some of the change they had left, Michael helped Anna to a stone seat against the outside wall of the Exchange. He looked down at the address he had written.

'What is it Michael?'

'My mother's address. Here in Cairo.'

'Your mother?'

'Yes. Frank gave it to me.'

'Oh. You didn't know she was here?'

'No. I haven't spoken to her for almost ten years. She walked out on my father. I was away at school.'

Anna winced as she moved awkwardly. She spread her palm over her left side and probed it gingerly.

'How are you feeling?'

'It's sore.'

Michael thought for a while and made up his mind. 'Let's go get some help.'

Another taxi and a journey via the Garden Hostel to another Egyptian street. This one, however, was tucked away in the leafy upmarket neighbourhood of Al-Maadi. The house was a single storey building set within its own walled compound and surrounded by lush planting.

Michael paid off the driver with the last of their money, digging out every last note and coin from his pockets. He carried Anna to the front porch. She collapsed onto a wooden bench. He rang the brass doorbell and after a few minutes a young boy opened the door. He stared at them with wide eyes before running back inside. They heard a voice call out, 'William, what is it?'

And in that moment, a woman in a white cotton dress appeared in the entrance. She looked at them, quizzically. Then with a sudden intake of breath she faltered and grasped the door frame. 'Michael?'

He nodded, not daring to speak just yet.

'Michael.' And then she rushed forward, put her arms around him and squeezed. After a few moments she let go and with a hesitant smile asked, 'Who's this?'

'My friend, Anna.'

Anna had stood up and slowly shuffled towards him. He quickly went to her side and helped her inside the house. 'She's hurt.'

His mother's face changed, and she became very serious. 'Bring her inside. What happened?'

'I had an argument with a concrete barrier,' Anna professed with a slight grimace.

'You have to fix her.' Michael knew that his mother had been a nurse. In fact, it was at the hospital in Oxford that she had first met his father. Well, that was the story he'd been told. His father had been hospitalised because of some respiratory infection he had picked up in Beirut.

'Michael, I haven't worked in a clinic for years,' his mother said exasperatedly.

'Please,' Michael asked.

His mother gave a little shrug and carefully helped Anna onto a couch. She asked Anna's permission to lift up her shirt. With quick hand movements she pressed the reddened area. Anna winced but didn't cry out.

'I don't think it is serious. The skin isn't broken. Luckily it isn't near the kidneys. However, I think a cold compress will help reduce the swelling.' She looked at Anna, 'Are you allergic to any medicine?' Anna shook her head. 'You will need to watch for blood in your urine. Painkillers will take the edge off the ache.'

The night passed whilst Anna slept on an ottoman couch in the living room. Paracetamol, ceiling fans and the drowsy heat had lulled her to sleep within minutes. Michael sat with his mother on a nearby sofa, questions wheeling about his head. His mother looked nervous. She hadn't aged that much from the way he remembered her — perhaps a few more lines around the eyes.

'How have you been?' she asked, haltingly.

'I got by. It was tough after Dad died …' Now Michael's voice left him and what he had to say tailed off into silence. His mother played with the tasselled cords of her dress. Then she moved to sit right beside him and took his hands into hers.

'It began almost fifteen years ago. I kept having these strange feelings. But your father refused to believe me. He thought I was making it up. To get attention. It was why he thought it better you go away to school. There was a man … a man, not really a doctor, still someone who knew what I was feeling. He helped, but your father didn't understand. But it got worse, and so I left. Eventually, with the right support … the right medication, my life changed.'

'How could you leave me?' Michael responded. 'Didn't you think I needed you?'

'I couldn't even look after myself. Besides, you had your father.'

'But Dad was always wrapped up in his work.'

His mother reacted defensively. 'Michael, you must realise that in spite of that, you put him on a pedestal,' she fired back. 'I couldn't compete with that.'

Whilst they were talking, Michael noticed a framed picture of his mother strolling arm-in-arm with a man.

'Who's this man?' Michael interrupted her, pointing at the photograph.

'Narek. My husband. He lifted me out of depression and gave me the courage to go on living.'

'What does he do?'

'Narek is the Trade Attaché at the Armenian Embassy here in Cairo.'

Michael's mother reached over and held his hands. 'Look son, I promise that I'll be a there for you as a mother from now on. I have battled with things you do not know … and probably don't want to understand. But that is in the past. Things have changed. I am stronger now.'

There was the crunch of gravel and the sound of a car door shutting. After a couple of minutes, a man in a grey suit appeared at the door of the room.

'Michael. This is Narek.' The man deftly nodded his head and walked over to them. Just then, there was a cry from upstairs. 'It's William,' his mother apologized and left the room.

Michael eyed the stranger, waiting for him to say something. But he didn't. 'Is he your son?' Michael asked nervously.

'No. What gave you that idea? William is our neighbour's child. They are travelling and couldn't take him with them.'

'Oh.' Michael's voice, clear with relief.

The man sighed. 'Michael, your mother never stopped caring for you. But she felt she could never win back your trust. Besides, she didn't want to turn your life upside down.' Narek was

161

very cultured and suave. His neatly trimmed beard and greying hair leant him an air of considerable sophistication emphasised by the expensive suit he was wearing. A huge contrast to his father, Michael thought. He always dressed in a Tweed jacket, shirt and knitted tie, preferably ones that didn't match. 'Anyway, what brings you here?'

'We needed help. We think someone dangerous has followed us from Arizona.'

'Why do you think he was after you? This man. An American, you think?' the diplomat asked.

Michael explained about finding the papyrus and going to Tucson to have it carbon dated. 'It led from one thing to another and now seems to come from a larger cache buried someone in the oasis of Siwa.'

Narek pondered for a while, deep furrows appearing on his forehead. 'It can only be for the papyrus. The reason this man is after you. Nothing else makes sense.'

'But it has gone. Destroyed. And in any way, there are only four people alive that knew it existed. Anna, me, the soldier's son and Frank.'

'It must be this person called Frank then,' Narek replied firmly.

'No. He couldn't be involved. Frank has always looked out for me.'

'Me too.' Michael turned around as his mother walked into the room. 'He was good at keeping me up to date with the things happening in your life.' She stood next to her husband.

'You say you've lost all your money?' Narek enquired.

'Mine was stolen. Anna's is in the gutter somewhere.'

Michael's mother pulled her purse out of a bag on the sideboard. 'Here. I think there's a few hundred dollars there. Also take this.' She passed him a plastic card. 'It's for an ATM and you can use it if you need to.' She then told him the security number. Narek pulled from his wallet a wad of local currency. 'You'll need this too. You say they were following you in a car. So, go by train to Alexandria or further on to Mersa. You can get a bus to the oasis from either of them.'

Anna woke shortly afterwards, her injury significantly better, and they took time to assess their situation. They had both lost their smaller day-sacks but still had larger backpacks, which they had brought with them from the hostel. They didn't lack for clothes but had lost wallets, water bottles, cameras and a first-aid kit.

Whilst they went on the hunt to replace some of these, Anna asked Michael, 'Do you think he … the American … still thinks we have it?'

'The papyrus?'

'Yeah.'

'Maybe he doesn't realise it was lost in the fire,' Anna said.

Michael thought about it for a moment and an idea suddenly struck him. 'We're going to have to have something to fob him off with.'

'Fob him off? What is it with you Englishmen and your archaic phrases?'

He smiled. 'Yes. You know, if he comes after us again, we can distract him. Trick him.'

'A fake?' She nodded approvingly.

They walked several streets over to the nearest shopping centre. It wasn't huge, but it had several souvenir shops, all selling the ubiquitous tourist trash. The second one had a substantial pile of modern replicas of pharaonic papyri. Michael went through them, carefully looking for ones with a finer weave and lesser printing. In the end, he approved of only two that he thought would be good enough for what he had in mind.

Next they went to a stationery shop and picked up penknives, bottles of brown and black ink and several fountain pens. Finally, at a small supermarket, Michael got a can of hairspray. Back at the house in Maadi, he set about cleaning off the existing images. He covered the papyrus with a coat of hairspray and waited for it to loosen the ink. Using a clean rag, he blotted the surface before repeating the process.

Anna inspected the blank sheets. 'Now what?'

'We are going to cut them down to the right size and artificially age them.' Trimming the pages and then using a wire brush to scourge the edges produced a suitably irregular piece. A rub with a used tea bag darkened it. Patting it dry with a napkin, Michael was ready for the next stage.

'What are you going to write?'

'I don't think it really matters. We only have to fool the people chasing us. They don't look like experts. But I'm going to copy out different lines from the original text and insert words I do know how to write.' In the end, the two pieces were not that awful. For his first attempt at a forgery, Michael was pretty impressed with the results.

Later, Narek drove them to the Ramses Railway Terminus. Michael's mother refused to come with them. She declared that it would be too emotional. 'One set of tears is enough for today. But you will come back and see me again?'

'Soon,' he promised. Seeing his mother had shaken his world. Michael tried to reconcile the two stories that he now knew, but it was going to take some time before he would be at peace with both. Michael also didn't know how to deal with the fact that Frank had been in contact with his mother all along.

The train station was a massive shock. The chaotic mass of people milling around was unbelievable. Michael couldn't tell where one queue began, and another ended.

'There!' Anna pointed at a sign with the word '*Alexandria*'.

Below it was a small window and behind this was a wizened man talking very fast and furiously with another. Notes and coins were exchanged, and the customer left with a paper ticket.

'Two tickets to Alexandria', Michael said, holding two fingers up and pointing at the sign.

'First class only,' the ticket counter man stated.

'No. That's too expensive. We can't afford it,' Anna chimed in.

'Anna. Look at the prices.' The fare for the various stations was pinned up against the glass. Michael pointed to the column that indicated First Class travel and ran his finger down to the station of Alexandria. It was blanked out, but below it was Mersa Matruh — forty odd dollars for a two-berth sleeping compartment.

She looked up at him with a smile. 'That'll do.'

Chapter 27

Oxford, England, present day

'What happened?' Frank stood in the centre of the Persian carpet that dominated his office at the Registry. Although he was very agitated, he consciously tried to control his impatience.

Smith lounged on a leather armchair near the window. 'The girl recognized Alex. They were at the bus station and they just took off.'

'Which station?'

'Does it matter?'

'Michael called me yesterday. He said he knew where the rest of the documents might be.'

'So?'

'He said it was in an oasis.'

'Egypt has so many.'

'I know. That's why I need to know which bus station.'

The thin man picked up his phone and proceeded to send a message. A minute later he got a reply. 'Turgoman.'

'Alright. Buses from there only go north into the Delta, west towards Alexandria or east to the Red Sea. For the Kharga, Dakhla and Bahariya oases you get the bus from Heliopolis. The only oasis to the west is Siwa.'

Smith sat bolt-upright, his face alive with interest. 'Good show.'

'Tell Alex to head there direct. Goddamn it. Tell them to back off. He doesn't need to scare them.'

'Frank, don't get so emotional.'

'Yes, well. Michael isn't our enemy. He is …'

The thin man interrupted. 'He isn't your son, Frank.'

Chapter 28

Mersa Matruh, Egypt, present day

The train with its cracked carriage windows rattled along the coastal rail line, its weary-eyed occupants stiff and motionless. Dawn had arrived and Anna and Michael rocked gently together as the carriage undulated over the uneven track. They were standing between the passenger cars in order to get some fresh air. Michael slid down the nearby door window and they were hit by a breeze from the sea — salty and yet somehow unsoiled.

Anna pulled him around and hugged him, her head on his chest. She looked pensively out over the turquoise blue water of the Mediterranean.

'What are you thinking?' Michael asked her quietly.

She gave him a crooked smile and replied, 'You won't like it.'

'Try me.'

'I was thinking how we are living in dangerous times. Maybe the most dangerous in human history.'

'That's dramatic. What do you mean?'

'Well. In the past, we didn't have the ability to destroy the world. Now we do.'

Michael looked at her curiously. This girl was remarkable. Her concerns weren't trivial.

'You name it: Nuclear war, biological pandemic, environmental destruction. All these could wipe us out,' she continued.

Michael nodded. 'Okay …'

'And then there's killer nature.'

'Killer nature! What's that?' he asked.

'Like a comet impact. That would do the trick. Or a super volcanic eruption. Or a basalt flood. They last for thousands of years. Either would send the climate into deep freeze.' She paused. 'We are increasing the chances of the former but are powerless to prevent the latter.'

Michael thought about it for a minute. 'Won't it just get worse?'

'Not really. In a few hundred years, I think we will have the capability to tame the more deadly aspects of nature. Maybe siphon off energy from volcanoes before they explode. Control long term climate and prevent biological holocaust.

Even now, we almost have the ability to deflect rogue asteroids.'

He pondered what she was saying. 'So it's a question of whether we can hold on for a few more generations. Until a more enlightened society emerges. One that can cooperate peacefully and solve global problems.'

'Yes. That's about it.'

'Fuck.' Michael said glumly. 'We're screwed, aren't we?'

The station at Mersa Matruh was relatively modern, but the long grey platforms were a stark contrast to the rusty carriages that filled the sidings. After getting off the train, Michael and Anna waited and watched the main street outside the station for ten minutes, but there was no silver SUV in sight. Then Michael decided they should walk the half mile to the bus station, which was south east of the town. The sky above was a glorious blue and the roads were almost empty. Michael felt a huge sense of relief when nothing followed them.

It took half an hour to find the right place and purchase tickets from a small hut on the roadside. A few older men in white kaftans stood nearby, tattered suitcases and well-used cardboard boxes in a pile next to them. A rotund driver in a blue shirt with a red logo over his breast pocket, came out from another building.

The men started to gather their belongings and moved towards a rather scruffy looking bus. The driver checked their tickets, and they clambered aboard. He looked at Anna and Michael. 'Ant dhahib 'iilaa al-Siwah?' he inquired. Michael nodded, and he took their tickets.

By the time they got on the bus, all the window seats had been taken. As they shuffled to the back, a young man quickly offered them his place with a simple gesture and they settled onto the hard seats. For the first few miles, they bumped and shook as the vehicle took them out along potholed roads towards the desert.

Michael pulled out the book on Siwa that Anna had discovered in Cairo and, whilst she dozed next to him, flicked through the first few chapters. It seemed the oasis had been settled for at least 12,000 years but only started to become noteworthy in the 7th century BC. Around this time, rulers were regularly consulting the Oracle. Even Alexander the Great journeyed there in 331 BC. Although it appeared that the priests of Amun held sway for another thousand years, their influence slowly declined. There was no evidence that Christianity ever reached the oasis, and only in the 11th century did it convert to Islam. The population of Siwa ebbed and flowed through the ages, reaching as little as forty men at one point. Now it was a bustling town of more than thirty thousand.

The young man who had given up his seat came and sat opposite them. He was a gangly individual, with several days' black stubble on his chin. 'Tourists?' he enquired. Anna, who had now opened her eyes, nodded but didn't reply. 'Going to Siwa?'

Michael thought this was obvious but nodded as well.

'Why are you going there? Nobody goes there anymore.'

Michael struggled to reply. Why was he really going? Now that it all was just that bit more dangerous. And why was he dragging Anna along? He thought about answering with some casual off-the-cuff remark but in the end opted for honesty. 'I'm not sure at the moment.'

The youth accepted this with a dip of his head as if not knowing what you were doing was entirely reasonable.

'How about you?' Michael asked back.

'I am going back to visit my family. We Egyptians belong to the place where we were born.'

Chapter 29

Siwa, Egypt, present day

The road was a ribbon in the desert — a grey stripe snaking across barren plains beneath whitewashed skies. Occasionally, they passed dust-covered trucks going in the opposite direction and once, a lone camel wandering aimlessly alongside the highway.

After some hours, the vehicle reached the top of a long ridge of sandstone and halted. It dwelled there for just a moment, hesitating. In a hollow that reached to the horizon was a dark mass of trees — an incongruous sight after the emptiness they had just passed through. To the left and stretching to the skyline were slivers of silver-blue, bounded in the far distance by jagged escarpments. 'The salt lakes of Siwa,' volunteered the young Egyptian sitting opposite them. Michael pushed open the sliding window next to him and immediately the bus was filled with an acrid brackish aroma.

With a spluttering engine, the bus took them down into the oasis and through dusty olive plantations. As they entered the settlement,

Michael noticed several massive stone mounds rising out of the trees a few miles from the road. They soon reached the main square and pulled up next to a mosque. Above the low-rise building, jagged fingers of an ancient fort loomed. The Shali citadel was a thirteenth century mud-brick fortress, hemmed in by tiny houses that had been substantially destroyed by heavy rains in 1926. Residents had fled from the destruction and it had largely been abandoned since then. 'Let's go find somewhere to stay,' Michael said as they climbed down from the bus.

'A wash and change. Yes, please,' Anna replied.

The hotel was a short distance away. They walked through a simple adobe gate, up a flight of tiled stairs and across a roof terrace that backed up against the ruined fortress.

After getting their room, Anna and Michael showered. The bathroom was simple, with bare plastered walls and unglazed terracotta tiles. They washed each other's bodies with care and attention and spent several minutes just hugging under the needle jets of water, until Michael remembered guiltily that fresh water was scarce in the oasis and shut off the taps.

Once they had finally got dressed, Anna picked up the Italian archaeologist's journal. 'You know this is one of those great tragic love affairs. Like Romeo and Juliet.'

'You know they were just book characters?'

'Yes, but still.'

Anna flicked through the pages and then scrutinized the archaeologist's entry on Siwa. 'These markings with the numbers above them. What do you make of them?'

'Mmm. I'm not sure. They don't seem to make any sense to me.'

Siwa was nestled between two salt lakes, on a strip of land barely three miles wide. The easternmost half was mostly given over to palm plantations whilst the western side was predominately made up of settlements that stretched along the roads that ran north and west. The main archaeological sites were on the eastern side and Michael decided that they should head there first.

'Ya basha!' called out an adolescent boy as soon as they stepped out of the hotel. He was riding a cart pulled by a scruffy-looking donkey. 'Cleopatra's pool, Mountain of the Dead.'

'No need. La! Shukran,' Michael shook his head to emphasise this.

'You know it's almost two miles to the Oracle?' Anna looked at him bluntly. 'And it's hot.'

'Right.' Michael peeled off a ten dollar note and flashed it to the boy. 'You take us where we want to go? For the whole afternoon?'

'Of course, ya basha.' The grin on the boy was infectious, and they both climbed aboard the creaking contraption with smiles on their faces.

'To the Temple of Amun, then,' Michael instructed.

Soon they left the town behind them and entered an area of thick vegetation. The donkey clip-clopped his way along the dusty road as it meandered up and down. After a while, the donkey turned left onto another track. It looked like it knew the way, for the little boy neither pulled on the reins nor gave it a command.

Within minutes, they came across a wide circular pond lined with a stone wall and filled with water of a curious green colour. 'Cleopatra's spring,' the boy stated proudly. The donkey by this time had come to a halt outside a tent-like structure with a bar and several chairs nearby.

'The Temple, not the pool,' Michael said exasperatedly.

'You no want to swim in pool?'

'No. The Temple,' insisted Michael.

With a glum face, the boy flicked a whip at the donkey, which reluctantly started to walk on.

The next open space they came to was the southernmost of the two main archaeological sites. 'There are two temples,' Michael read out from the guidebook to Anna. 'One is the Temple of Amun. The Oracle. The other is this one, the Temple of Umm Ubayda.' It honestly didn't look like much — a pile of large stone blocks and a few rocky outcrops.

'You stop here?' their young guide asked.

'Na'am,' Michael confirmed. They clambered down from the cart and strode up to the top of the mound. Michael couldn't discern any layout to the Temple. It was as it first looked, a random pile of blocks. They strolled around the site, ending up on the far side.

As Michael looked northwards, Anna came and joined him. Without realising it at first, he found he had slipped his hand into hers. She squeezed it and moved closer to him. The sun was dipping towards the horizon in the west and a bronze light burnished crumbling stone walls rising up above the palms. The Temple of Amun was perched on top of the small yet steep hill, its sides heavily weathered. Anna took out the copy of Hornemann's map and surveyed the ruins in front of them. 'There seems to be a lot less now than there used to be. His sketch of the Oracle has numerous towers and walls.'

Michael opened the travel guide once again and rifled through to the pages on the oasis. 'It says here that even in the 18th century the Temple compounds were fairly intact. But over the years much of the stone has been removed to construct other buildings in the oasis.'

'Well, let's get going.' Anna strode down the rise and headed back towards the road. They climbed aboard the donkey cart and Michael signalled to the boy that they should carry on.

Soon the Oracle was out of sight, hidden by the trees. They trotted passed row upon row of ragged date palms, the ground between littered with dry fronds. Anna was still holding the plan the German explorer had drawn, and she pointed to it now. 'It looks like the two temples were once connected by a causeway.'

'What does the guide book say about the Oracle?'

'Well, it appears to have been built just after 600 BC.

Michael looked over her shoulder. 'From the plan, it had a courtyard with an inner hall that led to a central sanctuary. There appear to be several small chambers surrounding that. I wonder if that is where he discovered the storage jar?'

The cart came to a halt at the base of the plateau. Michael gave the boy a few coins to encourage him to wait for them. Then he and Anna scrambled up the winding path and walked through the edifice. Michael was shocked at the state of the Temple. Apart from a few walls, constructed from large slabs of limestone, most of the structure was made from mud bricks. The tallest structure, a minaret, was clearly a more recent addition.

'On Hornemann's drawing, the position he marked with a cross is somewhere to the west of the Temple,' Anna remarked. She then took a circulatory route through a maze of low walls to the left side of the plateau. As she went, she said, 'We have to orientate the map with what's left of the structure.'

'It's not going to help that the Ancient Egyptians didn't have a consistent plan when it came to their Temple alignment,' Michael commented.

'I thought I read somewhere that they positioned the main axis towards certain stars.'

'I'm not sure where you got that information, but most were orientated towards the Nile. Very roughly in an east-west direction.'

'Well, we are a long way from the river.'

There were half a dozen people milling around on the far side. From the clothes they wore, Michael could tell immediately they were all locals. A father and his two young daughters were cavorting about, and there were a few young men taking photographs of themselves, posing on various rocks. Anna and Michael found a small promontory to stand on and compared the scene before them with what Hornemann had sketched.

Directly below them and to the right was what looked like a building site with an area of patchy ground mottled with half-built houses. To the left, a swathe of palms trees stretched as far as the eye could see.

'Where are you from?'

Michael spun about and took in the middle-aged man, the father of the two girls. He had a large triangular shaped head and a curious way of looking at him from out of the corner of his eye.

'England,' Michael replied slowly. The man didn't reply to this. So, Michael asked uneasily, 'How about you?'

'From here. I was born here, but now I live and work in Alexandria.'

'Do you miss this?'

'Of course. Some of these are my family's date farms.' He pointed to the west. 'They have been passed down the generations for hundreds of years.'

'It's a pity that the Temple has seen better days.'

The Egyptian rubbed his chin. 'Most of the ruins up here were built by the people of the oasis. They lived here before the new town was built.'

'What is that over there?' Anna asked, pointing to a yellow cone peppered with black dots on the horizon.

The Egyptian swivelled his head to see what she was pointing at. 'We call it Gebel el-Muwata. The Mountain of the Dead.'

'An ancient necropolis?' Michael enquired.

'Yes. But it isn't preserved well. You had better stay away from it at night.'

'Is it dangerous then?'

'It is, I believe, haunted. Whatever you do, do not wander alone at night. There are things … jinn … who take away those they find alone.'

Chapter 30

Siwa, Egypt, present day

Michael woke with Anna nestled up close against his back, her warm body spooning his. Michael didn't move, fearing it would disturb her. For several long minutes he listened to the sound of mice, scuffling around in the roof.

'Can we rest a bit today?' she quietly murmured. The words whispered in his ear — her voice groggy with sleep. 'Take a time out from the whole treasure hunting thing?'

Michael turned to face her, 'Sure.'

Later, as they wandered through the town, people stared at them. Not in an overtly threatening way, but obviously they were curious. Michael had pulled on jeans and a hoodie. Anna had dressed in joggers, a University of Arizona long-sleeved T-shirt and denim jacket, her hair pushed up under a baseball cap. They had discussed it earlier and thought it best not to draw too much attention to themselves. But clearly tourists were quite rare in the oasis these days.

Near to the Shali fortress, they passed a restaurant draped in vines and palm fronds. Outside, a man was barbecuing chicken on a charcoal grill. 'Hungry?' Michael asked Anna.

'Let's go for it.'

They took a table inside and ordered plates of chicken, falafel and baladi flatbread. The bread was ubiquitous across the country. Every neighbourhood had little kiosks selling the basic staple. It was common to see Egyptians queuing up early in the morning to buy a whole pile of them.

Afterwards, they meandered through the streets, occasionally coming across stalls selling hand-woven rugs or locally made jewellery. One of the pieces, an elegantly formed ring in gold, seemed to catch Anna's interest. She studied it for a while and then put it down.

'No? Not interested?' Michael asked.

She smiled at him before saying, 'We carry with us debris of unimaginable events.'

'Mmm?'

'Gold. A neutron-rich element.'

'That's one way of putting it. Not exactly the most romantic, though.'

Anna laughed, 'You wouldn't believe the reality.'

'Try me.'

'Gold probably isn't formed by the supernovae explosions I told you about. It needs to be bathed in neutrons.'

'Such as?'

'When two neutron stars collide.'

Michael waited. He'd got used to being out of his depth when Anna was explaining this kind of stuff.

'The event is extremely rare. Massive stars collapse at the end of their lives to become neutron stars. Those are stellar objects that are made of just neutrons. Effectively dead. It requires both stars in a binary system ... a star system with two suns ... to explode, collapse and collide to produce this pretty metal.'

The houses surrounding the crumbling fort were eerily deserted. Roofless and derelict, they were crumbling before their eyes. After a while, the ruins started to merge with newer buildings, packed close together. Washing hung on clothes lines stretched between the houses. But as they wandered through the alleyways, Michael realised that they had got hopelessly lost.

'Let's try and retrace our steps,' Michael said, trying to keep any worry out of his voice. 'I'm sure we'll get back to the main square soon.' But the buildings all looked alike, and he didn't recognize any landmarks.

'Money!' The cry gave him a start, and he turned around to see a little boy holding out his hand. An even younger boy next to him piped up, 'What's your name?' Smiling, the child repeated this several times.

Anna took out a few coins from her pocket and offered it to the boys. Michael wasn't sure if this was a good idea. The boys didn't go away. Instead, they kept on chanting, 'Money! Money!' A couple of others had now joined them. Michael put his arm around Anna and turned their backs to them. They started to walk away.

The airless streets started to narrow, bricked walls hemming them in. Michael could see Anna was nervous. She repeatedly looked back across her shoulder. What had been four or five kids had now grown to over twenty. Michael also noticed a couple of adults further back.

Something pinged off the wall next to him. Grit flew into his face. Then something else hit his back. Small stones were being thrown at them. Michael pushed Anna in front of him, using his body to shield her. There was a cry, 'Ajami!' Michael quickened their pace and started to take any available turn that he could.

'Up there,' he cried. On their left was a rough-hewn staircase, rising up to the roof of a house. At the top was a large flat space. As they fled across the roof, the crowd below spotted them. Boys began pointing and shouting. A few had willow sticks and waved them with obvious agitation.

In front of them was a small courtyard, a weathered wooden door the only way out. Michael pushed down on the lock and leant his weight against it. It didn't move. It was fastened on the inside. Behind them, a babble of voices and scuffling of feet heralded the arrival of their pursuers. Michael and Anna turned and faced the crowd.

Then the door behind was flung open and a bearded man leapt forward, a long cane in his hand. 'Emšu!' he yelled and swept the cane back and forth. The mob broke and ran. The young boys disappeared down the stairs and into the alleys within seconds.

The man turned and motioned them towards the open door with wide outstretched arms. 'I am sorry that happened to you. But you cannot hold it against them. They are unschooled.' His English was good, only slightly accented.

Michael and Anna walked through a narrow hall and into a dim white-washed room. The change in contrast was dramatic, and it took a while for their eyes to adjust.

'Come, sit.' The man indicated a wooden sofa strewn with cotton cushions. 'My name is Salfi. How about you?'

'I am Michael and this is Anna.' Before Michael could say anything more, their saviour disappeared down a dark hallway. After five minutes, he returned.

'Thank you,' Michael stated. 'For rescuing us.'

The man made a dismissive gesture. 'No. No thanks are required. You are our guests here. What happened, just now, is not usual. But each year more and more people come from Cairo to live here.'

'They bring with them ways that are not our ways.' The comment came from behind them. Michael and Anna turned to find a woman wrapped in a dark shift dress and red headscarf bringing in a tray from another room.

The man called Salfi, stood and introduced her. 'This is my wife, Tala.'

'Please,' she said as she transferred things from the tray.

The man passed Michael a white liquid in a small metal bowl. 'It's our way.' Michael picked it up and immediately recognized it as goat's milk. He sipped at the slightly pungent liquid. 'Why are you here? These are dangerous days,' Salfi asked.

Michael turned to face the man. 'Here in Siwa?'

He responded, 'Egypt in general.'

Michael shared a glance with Anna and then replied, 'My work involves Ancient Egyptian manuscripts and yet I've never been here.'

'Has it been very bad?' Anna voiced.

The woman observed them with weary eyes and said, 'We are tired of the chaos … the uncertainty.' She then returned to the kitchen and closed the door.

192

'I used to work for a Canadian company for several years,' the man remarked. 'They were trying to improve the water for irrigation. But it proved fruitless. There is too much salt in the ground.' The man rubbed his hands together. 'Now we do what we have to, to make a living. But prices keep rising and the politics gets more absurd.'

Later, as they took their leave, Salfi pointed out how they should go to get back to the hotel. The Siwan shook Michael's hand and muttered, 'My house is your house. If ever you need help, please come find me.'

Chapter 31

Siwa, Egypt, present day

It was late in the morning of the next day that found them walking along dusty tracks to the west of the Oracle Temple — the events of the previous day, little more than a bad memory. There were only a couple of asphalt roads that crossed the area, but they had found side paths that took them deep into the date plantations. But try as they might, they couldn't find any resemblance to the things Arturo had marked down on his simple map.

'This is hopeless.' The disappointment was clear in Michael's voice. 'Everything looks the same.'

'Let's go back to the hostel. Try again later. When it's not so hot. Maybe further north?' Anna suggested.

They wandered down the footpath, past lines of wizened trees. The heat was stifling and the air full of dust, kicked up by their boots. They had come to a slight rise, and ahead the ruins of the Shali fortress poked above the palm leaves. Anna stopped, retrieved a bottle of water and took a long drink. As she swallowed, she scanned the horizon. Michael stood still and watched her, sweat glistening on her face and neck. Then he realised she had stopped drinking and had fixated on something in the distance.

'Quick! Michael the drawing!' she blurted out.

'What is it?' he responded.

She fumbled with his backpack and pulled out the Italian's journal, opening it to the page on Siwa. Turning it this way and that, she held it out at arm's length and compared it with the view in front of her. 'See!' she commanded.

'No.' Michael didn't understand what she was trying to show him.

'These little shapes,' she indicated the little drawing that Arturo had inked at the bottom of the page. 'They represent these outcrops. Here in front we have the Shali fort. To the right, there is the Gebel al Mawta.' Next she swung the diagram to the left and pointed to the south-east. 'Then there are the three peaks of the Gebel Dakrur. Finally, here to the east is the Oracle of Amun.'

Michael could see, rising above the trees, a series of rocky markers. Sweeping left to right, the Oracle Temple perched on its rocky outcrop, the

Dakrur hills, the Shali ruins and finally the Mountain of the Dead. Now he got it, he nodded his head. He pointed at the journal and asked her, 'The numbers above them …?'

'Mmm, they are all below two hundred. Bearings or angles, I think.' Anna's voice betrayed her elation. 'We just have to match up these and where they intersect, we should have the location. Oh Michael, it's so exciting.'

'Well, you're the mathematics expert. Can you figure it out?'

'Yes. But we're going to need a proper map. A protractor and a compass too. Arturo seems to have measured the bearing of these landmarks relative to one another. Whilst …'

'Whilst he was surveying the farmer's land,' said Michael, finishing her sentence.

'Yep. Let's get back to town,' Anna ordered, pushing him back towards the main road.

Trying to find a protractor and a compass in the oasis was a tall order. The place could only boast one very small stationery shop and a few convenience stores. However, after searching the shelves of virtually all of them, they did manage to acquire both items. The map, although, proved to be considerably harder. The only accurate map they could find was pinned to the wall of the police station. Unfortunately, the scale wasn't right. The map covered the whole of the oasis and the surrounding region. They finally solved it after they got the manager of an internet café to search for a high-resolution satellite image of Siwa and print it on a large piece of paper.

Once they got back to the hotel, Michael left Anna to do her calculations and returned to the hotel lobby for more bottled water. However, the reception had run out, so he strolled outside to buy some at the nearby kiosk. As Michael paid for them, he took in the street scene. Parked up under a large ficus was their young erstwhile guide and his donkey cart from the previous day — the branches of the tree looming wide and its leaves casting deep shadows across the main square. He seemed to be engaged in an animated discussion with a man in a brown jacket whose back was turned towards Michael.

Then the boy grinned, and the man passed him something. He turned and pointed at the hotel. The man walked away, signalling with his hands. Another shape emerged from the shade of the tree trunk. Michael stood there stunned. It was the American from the bus station. He couldn't believe that they had been found. The two men now moved off and disappeared around the back of the square. Michael briefly thought about following them but thought better of it. Spinning around, he raced back to get Anna.

As he burst into the room, Anna immediately exclaimed, 'Michael, I figured it all out.' Her attitude was euphoric.

'Grab your things.'

'What?' Consternation flashed across her face.

'We've got to get out of here. I've just seen the American from the bus station.'

'Here in Siwa?'

Michael nodded his head furiously. 'Quick. Quick. I think he knows we are staying at this hotel.'

'Oh, Michael,' Anna sounded spooked.

He consciously calmed himself. It would do no good to scare her. 'Look. It's just a precaution. We'll find somewhere less central.'

Michael opened the closet and began to pack things into bags. Anna came over and started to help. Then she suddenly stopped.

'What's the matter?' Michael queried her.

'Don't take everything. Leave a few items.'

Michael didn't understand what she meant. 'Include the fake papyrus,' she continued. 'No doubt, he will bribe someone to get into our room.' She pulled out several clothes, a book or two from the bag Michael had just now packed and pushed them back into the drawer. 'Maybe it will satisfy him and he will leave us alone.'

Down the stairs they ran, through the lobby and out the back of the hotel.

'Where to now? Another hostel?' Anna asked.

Michael thought about the guidebook they had just left. Too late to go and retrieve it.

'Salfi's place. They'll only be keeping an eye on the hotel.'

'Brilliant,' Michael grunted as they emerged into a backstreet. 'He did offer, didn't he?'

Chapter 32

North of Siwa, Egypt, present day

The small twin-engine Beechcraft airplane rolled to a stop and after a couple of minutes the door at the rear opened and a set of stairs let down. Two men appeared at the hatch and clambered stiffly onto the tarmac. Apart from a single vehicle waiting just off the runway, there was nothing to be seen in any direction. No buildings, no control tower, no structure of any kind.

'Let's go. Our pilot has to return immediately,' the thin man instructed.

'Is this even a proper airport?' Frank retorted, picking up a bag that had just been thrown down from the plane.

'Apparently, yes. There is a military one north of here, but this is the only place a civilian plane can land.'

The two men walked slowly towards the waiting car. Smith finally pocketed the phone he had been checking, turned towards Frank and said, 'Alex has gone rogue. We can't rely on him now.'

A worried look crossed Frank's face. 'What do you mean?'

'He isn't answering my calls or messages. I regret to say he has probably allowed greed to cloud his judgement.'

Frank's brow furrowed in alarm. 'How dangerous is he? What can he do to Michael and the girl?'

'Well, he is ex-militia.' Smith confessed. 'He grew up in some backwoods Californian anti-government compound. His uncle was a client of mine, and I thought I could help him … re-adjust.'

'Can you trust him?'

'Who can you trust these days? He has been useful in watching people for me, running a few errands. But now he clearly has … gone off reservation, as the Americans love to say.' The thin man's tone turned grim. 'Also, and I don't mean to pour fuel on the fire, but the Egyptian driving for him. It turns out he is some kind of ex-Mukhabarat agent.'

'The secret police?'

'Mmm. Yes, a perfect storm. I don't think your kids will be able to resist them.'

Chapter 33

Siwa, Egypt, present day

The Siwan was out. But his wife let Michael and Anna in and invited them to sit and wait in the small living room. They'd had to bang on the door for a few minutes and shout their names through the crack by the door frame before she had cautiously welcomed them in. While they waited, she brought them mint tea and small biscuits. She then disappeared into a back room.

Left to themselves, they checked their things and repacked their bags. Anna spent a while looking at the richly embroidered tapestries that adorned the walls and then took to pacing around the room.

Finally, Anna stopped, looked at Michael and appealed, 'Let's summarize what we know about the papyrus?'

'Sure.' Michael thought for a while. 'Right. There seems to be a traceable history. I think a quantity of documents was first found in the oasis by Hornemann. Then it was buried for some time until discovered by an Egyptian farmer. A single piece ended up in the hands of the Italian archaeologist, Arturo, which was then kept by a British soldier whose son donated it to the Registry.' He paused and then continued, 'So, at least we can work out the fragment's provenance for the past two hundred years.'

'But what about before that?' Anna asked.

'Well the text is written mostly in Egyptian. Not Greek or Latin.'

'Apart from the name.'

'Yes. Simon. That part is in Aramaic,' replied Michael. 'However, to be quite clear about this, Aramaic isn't what you would call a single language. It originated in the Tigris Valley three thousand years ago and eventually spread across a region that spanned Egypt to Northern Iran. It had its peak around 300BC but then slowly declined as it was replaced by Greek. Many variations developed and diverged, so much so, that they could be almost considered different languages. By the 1st century it was confined to localised regions like Judea and Assyria.'

'So not Egypt?'

'Not countrywide, no. But some cities like Alexandria had a large population of Aramaic speaking people.'

'So, the two parts. One Egyptian and one Aramaic, are they connected?'

'Without more of the page, without more of the whole text, we cannot be sure. Papyrus was a costly item. Typically, it was used and reused many times.'

'So it is entirely likely that they could be two unrelated things?' Anna suggested.

'Yes,' Michael conceded. 'There is more of the old Coptic writing but it is a bit idiosyncratic. Something very unique to that particular scribe.'

'So we have to find the rest of the hoard?'

Michael nodded ruefully.

Then Anna abruptly sat down next to him. 'You know you never asked me?'

'Asked you what?'

'Why I agreed to come with you.'

'I …,' Michael started to say. Then he shook his head. 'No, I never did.'

'Well. In my mind, I had a decision to make. To help you accomplish something. Something that had virtually no chance of success. Or not. But if we did succeed, the outcome … well, it might change the world. As I saw it, I had nothing to lose. I thought there would be no downside to helping you. After all, what could be the worst thing that could happen? And yet, the world had everything to gain.'

Salfi returned mid afternoon. Within a few minutes, Michael had outlined their situation to him without revealing the existence of the cache of parchments.

'So these ...'

'Strangers,' Michael finished for him.

'These strangers are pursuing you? You are not sure why?'

'Not entirely. But we cannot do what we have to, with them in the background.'

'They scare me,' whispered Anna.

The Berber man stood up and paced up and down a few times whilst drumming his two forefingers in the air. He spun around and pointed at Michael, 'You say they have a car?'

'Yes. A big four-by-four.'

'The Egyptian who is with them? The driver. He is from Cairo?'

'I think so. That's where we first saw him.'

Salfi clapped his hands, 'Then I have it.'

Chapter 34

Great Sand Sea, Egypt, present day

The vehicle they were riding in was a ten-year-old Cherokee Jeep, dented and scuffed from countless journeys. They had been driving for over an hour now. Salfi had waited until late afternoon, then circled around the main square a few times. Michael had wound down his window so that he could easily be recognized. On the last go around, he caught sight of the silver SUV pulling away from the kerb and falling into place, a car or so behind them. 'That's them,' Michael confirmed to the Siwan.

Salfi took the northern road that skirted the Lake of Siwa and then headed west. The lake stretched calmly away southward, shimmering in the evening light. After a while, they passed the last of the palms, turned off the rough track and crossed into a dusty wilderness. The region was peppered with stone towers that had been carved into strange shapes by years of wind-blown sand. Michael could almost sense the ground rising as the jeep climbed up through passes in the escarpment.

'Michael, I forgot to tell you what I calculated.' Anna pulled out the satellite photograph, on which she had drawn several lines and arcs. He turned around in his seat to look at what she was talking about. 'See here, all the lines intersect at exactly one point. This has to be the place.' The jeep lurched sideways and she fell across the seat.

'That's great. All we need now is to lose the fuckers following us,' Michael murmured to her.

Salfi slowed, pulled over to the left and squinted into the fading light. 'They are still following us. Keeping their distance, though. I think maybe two miles back.' The Berber then swept a calloused hand across the horizon, 'This is a landscape of terrible emptiness. Sometimes this emptiness finds its way into your soul.'

'That's heavy,' mouthed Anna to Michael when he turned in his seat to check on her.

For another hour, the Siwan drove steadily on — the landscape stark and barren. Michael had always wanted to trek across a desert — see if he could find solace in the isolation. Seeing this emptiness, he wasn't sure he wanted to anymore.

Occasionally, a low throb could be heard, just on the limit of hearing, fading in and out. It was impossible to know from which direction it came. When Michael heard it for about the fifth time, he asked Salfi, 'What's that?'

'A helicopter. There's a military airbase north of Siwa. Uthman, it is called. They are hunting arms-smugglers. Libya is a mess right now. You can get almost any kind of weapon there.'

'Are we in any danger?' Michael asked.

Salfi turned and looked at him coolly, 'We live with danger every day.'

The terrain started to rise and undulate as they approached the beginnings of a plateau. Salfi twisted the rear-view mirror and studied the scene behind them. 'Now the fun begins,' he muttered. Almost complete darkness had settled over the desert with just a faint hint of vermillion on the western horizon.

Very slowly, Salfi turned the jeep in a long lazy arc and headed southwards. 'We will double back now. Lose your friends in this maze of ridges.'

Anna looked at him with a furrowed brow. 'Can't they just keep following us? Follow our wheel tracks.'

'We have just crossed a region of mostly bare rock. Our tyres won't leave marks here. It will be impossible to know in which direction we have gone.'

'What about our lights?'

'There is an ancient watercourse near here which links to a camel track. Once we make it to that, I can switch them off and we will follow it back home. Your enemies will most certainly end up in a ditch with no one to rescue them.'

It was a nerve-wracking time for them — the vehicle slowly creeping along the dried-up wadi. Huge dunes reared up on either side. There was no sign of their pursuers. Salfi frequently stopped, looked and listened for any sight or sound but sensed nothing. A thin crescent moon had risen, but it was still a challenge to spot boulders or ditches that might bring their return trip to a very sudden end. Nevertheless, the Berber took it in his stride and even began to hum a low melodic tune to himself. Soon the ground eased and Michael finally let out a long breath. He released his grip on the door handle. Michael hadn't realized, but he had been crushing the life out of it for the last half hour.

'Thank good…,' was all he had time to say when a bright light shone in his face. A curse erupted from their driver's mouth and he wrenched the steering wheel over and accelerated. In front, the two enormous headlights that had painted them with such garish light disappeared to the right. Salfi switched on his lights. They bumped and lurched as the vehicle took off over the uneven ground. The noise level went through the roof. Michael started to shout. Anna too, but it all was lost in the cacophony of sound that enveloped the cabin.

Up and down through the gears, the Siwan racked his jeep, trying to stay ahead of their pursuers. However, the big four-by-four behind them was gaining ground. In desperation, Salfi swung up onto the rising wall of the dried-up river bed — the vehicle absurdly pitched over until it reached the top.

Salfi then pushed the jeep hard along the crest of the dune. Sand exploded at the windscreen, blotting out the view. The SUV was right behind them, its headlights pinning them in their beam. Salfi jinked the wheel and without warning turned off his lights, swinging the vehicle in a sharp turn. Then suddenly, the end of the world came and a thunderous roar shook the ground.

A black Apache gunship flew up over the jeep and banked fast and hard to the right. It must have manoeuvred through the wadi and then rose up the sand wall to catch them. Behind, the SUV had stalled and came to a halt on the side of a ridge, its beams directed skywards. Michael could see doors opening and someone started to step down. Then the front of the car exploded as its engine was pummelled by 30mm rounds from the helicopter — red tracer rounds lancing through the bonnet.

'Shit!' Michael thought he cried in a long drawn out howl.

Their jeep wasn't moving either now. They just sat staring in horror as the darkness settled over the scene. The bullets had cauterized the Land Cruiser — the glow from their impact fading as they watched in horror. Overhead, the helicopter made another pass. It briefly hovered over the scene. A searchlight flicked on and bathed the wrecked vehicle. Nothing moved inside. Then without another shot, it turned towards the east and within a minute had disappeared. All that Michael could hear was the clicking of cooling metal and the crackle of melting plastic. The acrid smell of burning rubber caught in his throat.

Salfi leaned forward and flicked a switch on the dashboard. Dust swirled in the beam of the headlights. They all looked slowly at each other, stunned and speechless.

Then abruptly, Michael's door was pulled open, and he was yanked outside. He fell to the dirt and rolled over several times, pain shooting through his shoulder and legs. He started to rise, but a boot pushed him down.

'Keep still, bud,' came a grim voice out of the dark. Michael struggled onto his back and watched a tall man step into the light. He took out a cloth and started to wipe something off his face. 'Goddammit. That hurt.' He had a laceration above his eye. The Siwan driver now reacted and started to clamber out of the car.

'Oh no. You just stay where you are.' The American waved something towards Salfi and he immediately stopped.

Anna cried out, 'He's got a gun, Michael.'

The American called out, 'Gethan, how's our driver?'

From out of the dark, Michael heard the sound of retching. 'Fuck, Alex. He's dead. He's got a hole in his chest.'

'Come over here. Keep this trained on them.'

Another man appeared out of the gloom, holding the back of his hand to his mouth. Michael recognized him as the tourist he had seen at the Coptic Museum back in Cairo.

'Sure man but let's go.'

Alex walked back to the smouldering SUV, reached into the back and pulled out a hefty device with handles and an LCD screen. 'Wait a minute. I want to pick up the drone.'

'Hurry up. It might return,' the other American urged, gesturing towards the direction the gunship had gone.

'Look, it's a thirty kay job. I ain't leaving it out here.'

'Cum'on Alex.'

'Two ticks. I just gotta spin the thing up and bring it home to papa.' Alex flicked switches and watched the screen.

Shortly a buzzing sound could be heard and within a minute the drone dropped to the ground in front of the jeep.

'This is how you followed us?' Michael slowly got to his knees.

'Yep. Thermal imaging. It's also got an auto land and a follow-me function.'

Anna stammered, 'Michael, are you okay?'

'Missy, you just keep quiet.' The American went over and took the pistol from his partner. 'Grab the Egyptian's rifle,' he commanded. His partner skirted around to the rear of the wrecked SUV, lifted an AK-47 from inside the trunk and swung it over his shoulder.

Anna had backed up, moving as far away from the gun as possible. Cautiously, the American poked his head inside the cabin.

'What do we have here?' Alex pulled the satellite print Anna had marked up from the back seat. She made to grab it back, but Alex swung it out of her reach. 'Whoa there.'

He looked it over, but any hope of him not understanding its significance was soon dispelled. 'Jackpot!' he cried.

'I don't think we'll be needing you anymore.' He signalled Michael to move away from the jeep. 'Okay, it's time to leave.' He clambered into the passenger's side, pointing the gun at Salfi and indicated they should go. 'Goodbye boy,' he growled. The other American got in the back.

'Michael!' The mournful cry came from Anna. But the jeep pulled away, and he was left alone in the darkness.

Chapter 35

Great Sand Sea, Egypt, present day

Michael tasted bile in his throat. He was on the verge of losing it. He bent over, put his hands on his knees and took slow deep breaths. This slowed his racing heart. He looked up. The sky was ablaze with stars. The moon had set. But he had no idea in which direction to walk. The lights of the jeep had disappeared and its tracks impossible to make out in the dark.

Michael wondered if he should wait for daylight. At least he knew the sun rose in the east. But was he south or north of the oasis? They had departed towards the west, but Salfi had driven in circles to confuse their pursuers. Then images of what might be happening to Anna played unbidden in his head.

Okay, he thought, he had to try. Trust to luck. The ground rose to the right, and he climbed the sand to reach the summit of the dune. He slowly turned around completely, scanning the line where the night sky ended and inky blackness of the land began. Very faint and far away, Michael thought he could detect a pinpoint glow on the horizon. He made a decision and started to walk towards it. Trust to luck — a mantra that would bring him to her.

The dirt was soft and made each step a struggle. It was so quiet that the whisper of sliding sand was all the sound he heard. This was the Great Sand Sea — an ocean of bleak nothingness. Michael vaguely knew it stretched beyond the border with Libya and halfway to Sudan. How many thousands of square miles he didn't know, but it was going to be huge.

Every frightening story he'd ever heard of, of people disappearing in the heat of the desert, came flooding into his mind. Then at that moment there was a muttering. It came from behind him and faded as it passed in front. Talking without words, he thought — Jinn. Spirits come to take him away, just as the Egyptian man had said. He slapped his face. He realized that he was scaring himself.

Throughout the long night, he staggered through a world drained of colour, frequently stumbling. Often the ground would fall away or the soft undulating sand would suddenly change to rock. His knees took the brunt of these falls, but one time he smashed his head against a large stone and lay stupefied for several minutes.

Rolling over, he levered himself up and got to his feet. Shaky legs carried him forward, and he continued his desperate mission to rescue Anna. All thought of finding the papyrus-filled pots gone.

Chapter 36

Great Sand Sea, Egypt, present day

'Stoy!' A heavily accented voice shattered the silence. Michael lurched forward in the dark. 'Wakef! Stop, I said,' came the voice again. Michael collapsed onto his knees, his heart thumping.

Abruptly, someone pushed him fully to the ground and thrust his face into the sand. Hands roughly patted him down. 'Chisto,' the same curt voice sounded again.

Michael jerked his head up. 'Who the fuck are you?' The words were out of his mouth without thinking.

'Well, I could ask ze same about you?' a strong Slavic accent boomed out of the blackness. Torch beams flicked on and dazzled Michael's eyes. He covered his face and peered between his fingers.

'Okay. Get up,' barked another. This accent was less guttural. In front of Michael were four soldiers, kitted out in black webbing, vests and helmets with night-vision goggles. They were all pointing assault rifles at him.

'Who are you?' One of the soldiers pointed at him.

'Michael. My name's Michael.'

'What are you doing out here?'

Michael's reserve broke. 'What the hell do you think I'm doing?' he yelled. 'Out on a midnight stroll!'

'Watch your mouth.'

Michael's anger lessened. 'Our vehicle was car-jacked,' he said more calmly. 'And they've abducted my friend.'

'By who? Who did this?'

'A couple of Americans.'

'Not Arabs?'

'No. White Americans.'

With the realization that he was harmless and not part of any terrorist gang, three of the soldiers moved away and started to check their weapons.

'Look. I've really had a shit day. Can you help me?' Michael pleaded with the remaining one.

'We can't help you. We have our own mission.'

'Please.'

The blackened face looked at Michael, impossible to read in the faint light. 'We are tracking a group bringing out Iglas. They left Libya and are going west, then south. Probably heading towards Sudan.'

'Iglas?' Michael queried.

'Surface to air missiles. Stingers.'

'Are you Russian?'

'What makes you think that?'

'Stoy is Russian for stop.'

'Yes, well let's not get into that. In spite of what you hear, our countries do collaborate to hunt terrorists.' With that, he strolled over to his men and started issuing orders. In Russian, Michael noted.

Finally, he'd had enough. 'Oi!' he shouted at them. 'Can I go now?'

As a group, they returned. 'Where are you heading?'

'Siwa.'

One of the soldiers faintly shook his head, 'Nyet. Siwa is in that direction.' He pointed somewhere over Michael's shoulder. 'You've been heading towards ze border.'

'No. The glow …?' Michael's voice spluttered to a stop.

'Ah. Over there?' the soldier gestured with his chin.

'Yes.'

'That's an oil refinery in Libya. One of ze tank farms there has been burning for a few days now.'

'Oh.'

'Siwa can't be seen from here. It's a hundred metres below us.'

Michael's legs gave way, and he sank to the ground, a whimper expelled from his lips.

'Why?'

'Anna.'

'She your girlfriend?'

Michael nodded. 'She was taken by the American. He wants something we found at the oasis.'

'Which was?'

Any shred of secrecy had evaporated. 'The first-hand account of a Jewish zealot.' At this mention, the tallest Russian looked up sharply. 'Probably from the first century,' Michael added.

The tall soldier started to say something, but the one who was obviously in charge silenced him with a hand signal. This same commander then ordered, 'We will sleep here and evac tomorrow. I will decide what to do with you then. Most likely we will take you to Sidi Barrani.'

Fear rose in Michael. 'No. No. I need to get back to Siwa,' he yelled.

'You have no say.' Michael started to answer back, but the soldier slapped him. 'Stop this.' The commander pointed to another one of his men, 'Bind his ankles. I don't want him wandering off.'

Michael was given a blanket and told where to lie down, his legs zip-tied together. The temperature had dropped, but it wasn't particularly cold. He lay still, hoping that sleep would come, but his anxiety about Anna and the hard ground made it fitful and exhausting.

Sometime during the night, Michael came awake for the hundredth time. But he kept himself still, not daring to think about the present. Trying to remember better times — like walking with Anna along the streets of Rome or the faint scent of oranges on her fingers after she had peeled and fed him segments on the bus to Siwa. In the background, Michael could hear the soldiers murmuring to one another. Their voices just a whisper but as he listened, allowing the sound to lull him back to sleep, he registered the words, 'ma ha-sha-a?'

Michael's eyes opened immediately. That was Hebrew. He flung off his blanket and turned to face them. 'You're Israeli! You're not Russian.' Michael's statement was like a bombshell. Everyone was up.

'You some sort of multi-lingual freak?'

'Something like that,' Michael spat.

The unit leader scowled at two of his soldiers.

'Slicha,' one of them offered. 'I thought he was asleep.'

'What are you? IDF?' Michael accused the commander.

'Something like that.'

The IDF was the Israeli military. Michael's father had encountered them several times in the past during expeditions to the West Bank. He considered them ruthless.

225

'Well the cat's out of the bag now. Israeli soldiers operating inside Egyptian territory!' The commander turned to his team, poised to bark out an order. 'Look. I too am on a mission,' Michael babbled quickly — rushing to fill the space, rushing to pre-empt his decision. 'To save my girl.'

The man swore. But then he remained silent for a while and appeared to mull over the situation.

'And to find the writing of the zealot,' Michael added.

The Israeli's face filled with tired resignation. 'You had better talk to the Rabbi.'

'Rabbi?'

'Yes. Their nickname for me.' The tall soldier came over and looked down at Michael. 'Tell me more about this account? About a zealot?'

'Not just any zealot. Simon the Zealot.' Michael then added, 'Maybe.'

With a quick nod to his captain, the soldier cut Michael's restraints and pulled him up.

'Why do they call you that? You really a rabbi?'

'No. But I attended a rabbinical seminary once. The others found out and …' He gave Michael a slight shrug. 'But you can call me Isaac.'

Before long the rest of the squad settled down to rest with only Isaac left on guard duty. Michael sat up and chatted with him, anything to keep his mind fully occupied. 'You worried the missiles will be used against you?'

The Israeli commando looked at him resignedly. 'Yes. We have many enemies. It has ever been the case.'

'When did it all go south for the Jews?'

'Go south?'

'Turn bad, then.'

'You've spent too much time with Americans.' He kicked at a small mound of dirt. 'It started long ago. Ancient history. But the beginning of the end was when the Romans invaded in 63BC. They created a puppet state ruled over by a puppet king. However, there was always simmering resentment. It flared up in 46 and then sporadically until a full revolt occurred in 66. The Romans brought in the legions from the north, but at Beth Horon their army was massacred by the Jewish rebels. After this, the Romans extracted a terrible retribution, crushing the revolt and razing Jerusalem and its Temple to the ground. Those captured were crucified or sold into slavery. Another failed rebellion in 132 guaranteed the total destruction of the Jewish nation. Its cities annihilated and its people dispersed.'

'That's brutal.'

'You have no idea.'

'Did the Zealots ever come to Egypt?'

'For sure. There are accurate historical records that chronicle their flight from Israel after these events. Some seeking refuge in Alexandria. Others further away like Thebes.'

Michael acknowledged this with a nod.

'So finding some evidence of them in Siwa isn't as strange as you might think,' said the tall Israeli. He looked at Michael thoughtfully and continued, 'I do not have your beliefs but I for one would wish to read what a Zealot from those early times had to say.'

Dawn arrived quietly a few hours later, the sky slowly brightening from the east. As the rest of the unit packed up their gear, the commander approached Michael. 'I have changed my mind. I will let you go. You are no threat but I want your word that you will never mention this.'

Michael nodded. If it allowed him to get back to saving Anna, he would agree to anything.

'I need someone to take him back to the oasis,' the Israeli captain inquired. He raised an eyebrow towards Isaac who stood next to Michael.

'Yeah. I'll volunteer.' And then the soldier slapped Michael on the back. 'Come on, little man.'

They trekked a few miles over stony ground until they came to a cliff with a crumbling scree slope. Several black openings hinted at caves behind. Into one, two of the unit disappeared and within minutes wheeled out motorbikes — each one a bit beat up but seemingly militarised versions of ordinary dirt bikes.

The commander pointed at the Rabbi. 'You have one day, then we depart. Drop him and rendezvous with us at the EP. 2400 hours tomorrow.'

With an afterthought, he uttered, 'Leave your weapons. You are just another crazy tourist biking through the desert.' Isaac stripped off his outer uniform, leaving just a faded purple t-shirt and his black fatigue pants.

Michael pointed to the bikes. 'How do these work?'

'They are off-the-shelf Metisse models. Though the suspension has been beefed up and they've added extra air filters.' He threw a leg over the seat. 'Let's get going.' Isaac kicked the starter pedal and twisted the throttle. A subdued growl came from the engine. 'Muffled exhausts too.' Michael climbed onto the pillion seat and grabbed hold of some webbing straps. Without another word, Isaac opened the throttle, and they shot off towards the rising sun.

Chapter 37

Siwa, Egypt, present day

Frank surveyed the manicured trees and elegant villas of the Shali resort. It was hard to believe they were in the middle of the Great Desert and in a country where much of the population was struggling to rise above the poverty line. Behind the sprawling complex rose the mountains of the Gebel Dakrur, angular slabs of rock formed out of layers of white limestone.

Smith stepped out of the room and onto the balcony. He pointed at the hills. 'I've always wondered if this is where the Ancient Egyptians got the idea of stepped pyramids from.'

Frank watched the man pull a cigarette from a pack and light it with a wooden match before replying. 'Like the ones at Saqqara? Yes, I do see what you mean.' There was much speculation where the original shape of the pyramids had come from. Was it an evolution of a single slab mastaba, to three or more layers and then finally to a perfect triangle? Or some other more natural inspiration, like the diverging rays from a clouded sun or the shape of a sacred hill?

'Alex has been in contact,' remarked the thin man.

'He's here?' queried Frank.

'Yes. He has the location of the papyrus cache.'

'Michael?'

'He has the girl. She is going to cooperate with us to …'

'Where's Michael?' Frank interrupted.

'He is alive. Unhurt, from what Alex says.'

'What's going to happen next?'

'We are meeting up with Alex later. A public place in the centre of town. He wants to agree terms. I am afraid he holds most of the cards at the moment.' The thin man stated, 'I'm sure it will all work out. Just another day. We will find the Zealot's story. The boy and girl will go back home. Maybe a little battered, but with plenty to talk about. The Americans will get their money. Eventually.'

Frank swore softly and sat down.

'Alex needs us. He doesn't have the access to the antiquities market that I have. He has agreed to let us copy any documents first and when they are sold, he will take sixty percent.'

Frank fidgeted in the chair. 'The Lost Gospel of Simon the Zealot?' he said pensively.

Smith thought about that for a moment. In order for it to be lost, surely it would have had to be known before? This was so far out of the expected that its discovery could change everything.

Chapter 38

Siwa, Egypt, present day

Salfi's house became a refuge once again. Isaac and Michael had arrived uneventfully in the oasis, just after noon. Michael suggested that they try to get help from the Berber once more. If he refused, and that was a strong possibility, then Isaac suggested they lie low in some derelict building on the outskirts of town.

However, when Salfi opened the door, he was visibly relieved. He confessed his conscience had been heavy with worry, fearing that Michael had died out there in the desert — that and the fact that the Americans had dumped him on the edge of the oasis and taken the girl, along with his vehicle.

He was very suspicious of Isaac. Michael had introduced him as George, a Ukrainian biker who was doing the Oasis Circuit — a route that took in all the five major oases and was the ultimate desert road trip. But he welcomed him with the usual Berber hospitality and let him wheel his bike inside the backyard.

As the muezzin sang out the call to prayer later that evening, Isaac and Michael sat around the dinner table and discussed their rescue plan. It all hinged on knowing where the Americans would be and that was the location Anna had worked out and that Michael had no clue of.

'You say the place is determined by a set of numbers?'

'Yes. But my girlfriend worked it out and I don't have the map.'

Isaac lifted his rucksack up from the floor, pulled a tablet from out of a protective sleeve and powered it up. 'What were the coordinates of the location?'

'They weren't coordinates as such but angles to certain landmarks.' Michael closed his eyes and tried to picture the page in Arturo's journal. 'I think I can remember them.'

The soldier had already brought up a detailed image of the oasis. He looked at Michael in expectation.

'The first point is this one,' Michael said, pointing to the Mountain of the Dead. Isaac used a stylus to add a red triangular marker. He repeated it for all the others Michael indicated:

the fortress, the Oracle and the Dakrur mountain. Then he created another green marker symbol and connected it to the four triangles. To the right of the screen, a box appeared with angle values. As he used the stylus to move the green symbol around, the angle values varied. 'All set,' he confirmed.

Michael gave him the values he recalled from the journal. Swiftly, Isaac keyed in the measurements. The green symbol immediately sprang to a particular point, a little way west to the Temple of Amun.

'That seems just about right,' Michael concluded.

'What weapons do they have?'

'At least a pistol and a rifle.'

'Make? Model?'

Michael thought about it for a moment. 'Something like a Glock and a Klashikov.'

'Kalashnikov.'

'What do you have?'

'Nothing. You heard my commander. No weapons. Not even a knife,' the Israeli soldier muttered in a hushed tone.

Salfi came into the room bringing with him a tray of food. 'Why so sad?'

'We are going up against some armed and very dangerous people,' Isaac replied, his Slavic accent more pronounced. He was actually Russian, he had told Michael. His parents had been part of the exodus of Jews to Israel following the collapse of the Soviet Union.

'We?' Salfi looked up sharply whilst pouring out three cups of tea.

'Yes. George has agreed to help,' Michael confirmed with a quick glance.

'Isn't that good? More is better.'

'Yes. But we don't have any weapons,' Isaac protested.

Michael added, 'We don't have anything to protect us.'

The Siwan nodded thoughtfully. 'I think I can help with that,' he muttered, slowly scratching the stubble on his chin.

Chapter 39

Siwa, Egypt, present day

Frank inspected the satellite image Anna had marked up and then surveyed the scene. The ground in front of him was free of palm trees for the most part — a patch of scrubby land that was slightly raised above the surroundings. The Oracle Temple was perhaps five hundred metres away to his left. 'This is where it is supposed to be buried? The pots that you say contain the parchments.' Anna stood behind him, sullen and quiet. One of the Americans loitered nearby.

Alex prodded her with a gun. 'Speak up missy.'

'Yes,' she said reluctantly.

Frank looked at her with a mix of feelings. 'Nothing more exact?'

'No.'

'It's like blood from a stone,' Alex declared. 'Let me have a few minutes alone with her and I'm sure she'll sing.'

'No!' Frank commanded.

'Old man. Hasn't it reached your head that you're not in charge?'

'Gentlemen. Let's not bicker amongst ourselves,' the thin man's unctuous voice soothed. He paced around in a small circle, tapping his fingers together, before he looked up and said, 'If only we had a thermal camera.'

'How would that help?' Alex questioned.

'Buried stones … pots, heat up differently to loose soil. They retain it much longer and so should appear hotter than their surroundings.'

The American slapped his leg. 'I've got just the thing. An infrared camera on a UAV.'

Smith gave a crooked smile and nodded his head in approval. 'Fly your drone over the area and let's see what it reveals.'

Alex strolled back to the jeep and pulled the aerial vehicle out from the boot. He flicked a few switches, peered at the display and put it down on the ground. The propellers started to spin up, and it quickly lifted into the air.

The thin man spoke to Frank, 'It's a good time. The sand hasn't had time to warm up.' Actually, the sun had only just cleared the horizon and there was a distinct chill in the air. It was a beautiful start to the day, with crystal clear skies and a few filaments of cloud high up in the stratosphere, catching the light and turning a pinkish gold.

For several minutes, Alex flew the mini-helicopter across the terrain. He kept it low and had the camera angled straight down. Smith watched the display intently. For the most part it was almost black with only a few reddish blobs.

Frank grabbed Anna's wrist and pulled her to one side. Very quietly, he hissed, 'I am going to walk you towards the car. Once you are there, you can make a break for it through the trees.' There was no response from the girl. He shook her arm. 'Got it?' Anna gave him a petulant nod.

'There. Go back.' Smith remarked.

The drone circled back and then hovered over a slight mound.

'I make out two perfect circles. That them?'

'Yes. I think so.'

With that, the two Americans pulled spades from the Cherokee and walked over to the sand mound.

'Careful now,' called out the thin man.

Slowly at first, they pushed dirt away, shovelling it into a heap nearby. For some minutes they worked until sweat drenched their clothes. Then it was Gethan who struck something hard.

Smith came forward and took the spade from Alex. He scraped some loose grit away and revealed the top of an earthenware pot.

'Bingo!' cried the American.

Smith brushed the immediate area clear of sand with a small brush. He twisted what seemed to be a large pitch-covered wooden lid and looked inside. A brown piece of parchment fluttered in the breeze.

The two Americans who were looking over the older man's shoulder whooped and clapped each other on the back. But it all fell suddenly quiet when Michael stepped out from behind a tree.

Chapter 40

Siwa, Egypt, present day

Michael had arrived on the scene just as he heard the cry. Shadows had hidden his approach. The trees were packed so closely together that the dark ground was dappled by only thin slivers of light. Three men were stooped over a hole in the ground. Michael recognized the two Americans — one, the erstwhile tourist from the museum and the other, Anna's visiting lecturer. But the third man he had never seen before. He was much older and almost stick-like. There was no sign of Anna.

Michael surveyed the rest of the location. To the left was a broken wooden cart, tipped on its side and covered in dried up palm leaves. To the right, and further back, was Salfi's jeep, parked up in the shade of a fig tree and against a low mud-brick wall. A small building made from large stone bricks sat in the background. It was deathly quiet, not even the birds made a sound.

Michael walked away from the tree. The movement caught the attention of the thin man.

He said something and the other two men twisted around and faced him. The taller one warily scanned the trees behind him before a slow smirk appeared on his face as he recognized Michael. 'You're a hard one to lose.'

'I've come for the girl.'

'Yeah. You and whose army?'

'Ah. But I'm not alone!' Michael whistled loudly – the agreed signal. From behind the remains of the wooden cart, stepped a Berber warrior, resplendent in a silver breastplate, circular shield and a long curved sword. The figure looked like it had stepped straight out of the pages of a history book. Salfi even held a spear in his right hand.

The tall American appeared to double over. When he straightened up there were tears in his eyes. 'You have got to be kidding. Right,' he laughed.

'No. There's more!' Michael whistled twice. From somewhere behind and to the right of him, there was a loud crack. A whoosh and something pinged off the rock near the thin man.

'What the fuck, man.' Immediately the other American fell to the ground. The AK-47 he was holding swung up and aimed in the direction of the shot.

'Where's Anna?' Michael shouted. Two hundred metres away, he knew Isaac would be dropping the ancient musket. They had broken into the Museum of Siwa, two hours earlier. The antique gun had been one of only two firearms that had been on display. It was an original Berber moukhala, with a ridiculously long barrel and a flared stock, inlaid with silver. Three waxed paper cartridges of very uncertain functionality had also been discovered. Isaac had cleaned and test fired the gun. Unfortunately, the first cartridge failed. The second one had worked, but the shot had missed the target he was aiming for by several feet. Now Michael was just hoping the noise would be enough.

Meanwhile, Salfi had stripped a mannequin of a Siwan warrior from the 18th Century. Isaac was very nonplussed when he watched him don the armour. 'Are you sure Salah ad-Din here knows what he is doing? When he said he could help, I thought he knew an arms smuggler. I didn't realise we were going into such a one-sided contest.'

The tallest man didn't flinch at the gunshot.

Michael repeated, 'Where is Anna?'

The American looked to his left before replying, 'Somewhere safe.'

'You've got what you came for. Let her go and we will leave you be,' Michael called out.

At that moment, two people stepped out from behind the jeep. It was some distance away, but Anna was unmistakable. She blocked Michael's view of the other man, but thankfully she seemed unhurt. Then from the corner of his eye, he saw a strange shape leap up from a pile of dead palm fronds near the jeep. Michael knew it was Isaac, but the speed with which he had covered the ground was unbelievable. Isaac fell towards the man behind Anna.

The American on the ground caught his movement. Without warning, he fired the assault gun. The noise shattered the silence. Bullets raked across the jeep, shattering glass and punching holes in the doors.

Immediately, Isaac rolled away. Within seconds, he was on his way towards the shooter. Michael had dropped to the ground when the gun had gone off, but now he raised his eyes and scanned the scene.

There was a sudden shout from his left and he saw Salfi charging at the Americans, his spear stretched out in front of him and the shield raised high. The tall American looked dumbstruck as he tried to react to both attacks. He barely had time to pull a pistol from his belt and raise it to firing position. In that instance, Michael was on his feet and launched himself towards Anna and the other man. There was a clash of metal as Isaac and Salfi converged on the Americans. The pistol blasted, but Michael didn't turn around to look.

Chapter 41

Siwa, Egypt, present day

Frank sat up. Everything had happened so quickly. He was in the process of urging the girl to run for it when he heard the familiar voice of Michael. It seemed he was shouting. He spun around. He had to stop anything bad from happening. Then all hell broke loose. A monster erupted from the bushes and the world exploded in gunfire. And then there seemed a blank in his memory.

At last, shaking his head to clear the mist, he stared at the girl. A red stain flowered across her shirt, just below the collar-bone. 'You've been shot,' he said with surprise. He crawled over, crouched beside her and focused on the wound. He was at a complete loss as to what to do. He knew no first aid. But the girl was obviously in shock. She flopped about and her eyes fluttered. Frank held her arms and gave her a shake, 'Stay awake!' he commanded.

Slowly she came around and her eyes concentrated on him. She nodded. Then her gaze dropped to his chest. She screamed. He didn't understand why, but now he felt something pulling him down. He sagged as energy drained from his body. The girl pointed at him. He really didn't understand but allowed his eyes to follow her finger. Blood was oozing from his chest.

Chapter 42

Siwa, Egypt, present day

Michael tore across the ground towards the two figures lying in the dirt. 'Anna,' he yelled. Sliding to a stop mere inches from them, he reached out to grab her, but the man who lay beside her was terribly familiar. His face was covered in grit and his hair all awry. But it was unmistakeably, someone he knew.

'Frank?' Michael's mind couldn't process the information. He looked at Anna. There was blood on both of them.

'Michael,' Frank gasped.

'What are you doing here?' Michael struggled to understand.

'He's with them,' Anna croaked.

'No. No. No. No. No,' cried Michael. Torn by indecision, he switched his attention back and forth. 'This isn't supposed to happen.'

Frank groaned. 'I never meant it to go this far. I tried to protect you.' His voice wavered as he tried to catch his breath. He flopped back, exhausted, life flowing from him even as

Michael watched. 'Alex has the papyrus. He stole it from the lab.' A long pause, then with more insistence, 'I wrote it. It's not real. Wanted to use it to save the Registry. Don't let them close it down. Promise me!'

Michael, now with tears in his eyes, just nodded. Frank murmured, 'My boy, I am so prou …' Then he was still. Michael felt something, almost physical, leave him then.

Anna still lay in a contorted heap, so Michael lifted her up gently and moved her towards the shade. She moaned slightly as he did this. When it was done, he collapsed beside her. Her shirt was soaked with crimson.

'I guess this is the end,' she whispered. They sat with their backs against the mud wall. Legs and arms entwined. Dust covered their hair. Michael reached out with his hands to cradle her face. The touch caused her to look at him. Resigned eyes glazed with tears. 'I'm glad we're together.' She huddled closer, but he had no words to say. 'All we have is this brief time. I love you.' The declaration stunned him.

Time slipped by — an hour … maybe two. Or possibly it was just five minutes. A shadow crossed the sun. The bulk of Isaac loomed over them. Michael looked up at him. He wasn't sure what to say. Isaac knelt to inspect Anna; his hands tore open her shirt. Michael started to tell him to leave her alone but the soldier pivoted to examine Frank before coming back to them.

Michael's voice returned, 'Leave her be. Let her rest in peace.'

Isaac viewed him quizzically. 'She's not dying. The old man took the bullet. She just got what was left. After it passed through him.' As he assessed her injury, he continued, 'She's in shock. She'll survive, though. Believe me, I've seen plenty of gunshot wounds.'

'What did you say?'

'She'll live.' He balled up some cloth he had torn from Anna's shirt. 'Here. Press this against her wound. It'll hurt, but it will do until I can get her a proper dressing.'

Michael felt weak with relief. It wasn't going to end. Anna's eyes were closed. 'Did you hear that? You're going to be okay.'

'The old man's a goner though,' Isaac simply declared. He then left to retrieve a first aid pack from one of the paniers on the motorbike. Whilst they waited, Michael tried to brush some of dirt away from the wound in her skin.

Anna raised her head, a faint smile on her lips. 'Remember … I told you, I agreed to follow you because there was no real downside.' Suddenly, she lurched forward and coughed, blood spattering her hands. 'I'm thinking I've got to re-evaluate that.'

Isaac returned and set about cleaning and dressing her wound. 'There's a spent bullet fragment in there. But it can wait 'til we get her to a hospital. I'm going to give her some painkillers and antibiotics now.'

Michael could see she was going to be alright. The bullet had lost most of its energy passing through Frank. Still, it had caused enough pain to shock her system.

There was a terrific yell from behind. Isaac cursed, 'Fuck. You'd better go and see what's going on. I'll stay with the girl.'

Walking nearer to the mound, Michael saw the strange sight of Salfi, still in his outlandish gear, struggling to subdue one of the Americans. Although he had been trussed up, he was flailing about on the ground. The other one was bloodied and bruised, his hands and feet bound together with rope. The thin man was nearby. He clutched at his side and looked shaken.

Salfi finally gave his prisoner a blow with his shield, and the struggling stopped. He grinned wildly and then, raising his spear and shield, whooped into the air.

Chapter 43

Michael peered into the hole. The opening to the earthenware jars gapping up at him, reams of thin papery sheets stuffed haphazardly inside. Kneeling down, he lifted the topmost bundle. It was clearly an early version of the book — a codex made from multiple leaves of papyrus, held together with a cord of leather, written only in the same familiar spidery Coptic hand, it seemed.

Suddenly, the thin man grabbed hold of Michael's arm, his bony fingers digging into his flesh. 'There is a hidden truth in this world. This could be it,' he wheezed. 'The actual words of God.'

Michael wasn't sure what the thin man meant by this, but he wrenched his arm away. 'It's a fake. Frank admitted it to me. He did it to keep the Registry going.'

'No,' the thin man moaned. 'It cannot be.' But Michael's words seemed to deflate the man. He fell back and appeared to diminish.

'What did he mean by that?' Isaac was there at Michael's side. He picked up the black slab of the pistol that had been flung to the ground in the mêlée.

'Anna?'

'Resting. She's good.' Isaac pointed at the thin man who by now was staring at Frank's body. 'So what did he mean?'

'They … or maybe just him. He thinks these texts are the secret sayings of God.'

Isaac eyed Michael thoughtfully. 'Well. I'm not sure if the world is ready for this knowledge. I think we might be better off not knowing.' The soldier pulled back the slide on the Glock and chambered a round. Michael froze as he understood his meaning. Isaac's expression was blank — his mouth grimly set. Then a huge grin exploded onto his face. 'Nah. Just kidding.'

Michael stared at Isaac with a stupefied look, then he swept a hand over his face and grimaced. 'What are we going to do with them?' He indicated the three bound men.

Salfi prodded one of the Americans with his spear. 'I think we'll let the local police handle them.'

'This one shot Frank,' Michael stated matter-of-factly, pointing to the shorter of the Americans.

Michael limped back to where Anna lay. 'You feeling better?'

Anna peered up at him, 'Yes. Your friend here seems to know what he's doing. Who is he anyway?'

'A long story,' muttered Michael. He looked over at Frank.

Anna saw this and reached out to touch his hand. 'Do what you've got to do.'

Half an hour later, Michael watched the taxi pull away, taking Anna to the local hospital. Isaac accompanied her and promised to take care of the girl until he arrived. From there, Isaac would reclaim his motorbike and then make for his rendezvous point. Salfi had taken the others to the nearby police station. A distant uncle of his was the deputy chief. Isaac had helped him get them into the vehicle and secure them with excessive amounts of duct tape. Before leaving, Isaac gave Michael a bear hug and fist pumped Salfi.

Michael wanted to do one more thing. He stooped down and lifted Frank's body. It wasn't easy, but he wasn't going to leave it out in the open, out in the sun, at the mercy of wild animals. The stone building had been a storehouse at one point. There were rough-hewn tables pushed up against the back wall. Michael laid Frank's blood-soaked body on one of them, folding his arms across his body and straightening his legs. Then Michael looked down on him, searching for the right thoughts — deciding how to frame his memory. For five minutes, he stood there, and then turned to leave.

Michael walked out the door and into the soundless world — from dark to light, from black to white. It felt like a rebirth. He tarried briefly on the threshold, aware of the significance of the moment. He had a purpose now, a cause as formidable as that of any zealot. As he walked away, a trail of vermillion drops fell from his fingers, like little tears.

Epilogue

The laboratory hummed with the sound of equipment. A technician adjusted the spectral analyser and scanned the document. Immediately it appeared on the adjacent monitor, the faint writing now in vivid contrast. He pressed a few keys and the image recognition program started. The machine translation software engaged and almost at once a rapid display of the text showed up on another monitor.

'That's the last one?'

It had taken six months to develop the AI algorithm and now the fruits of this labour were showing results. Full permission from the Egyptian Antiquities Authority had been given to analyse and catalogue the find in collaboration with several notable academics, including Dr Falisha of the Coptic Museum of Cairo.

'Yes. It's done.'

'So only the Aramaic was forged. Tagged onto the original Egyptian text.'

X-ray microscopy had revealed that the ink used to write the Aramaic text contained substantial amounts of modern contaminants.

'Yes. Samples taken from several pages and even from the leather thongs that were used to bind the bundles together … all were carbon dated to the early part of the first century. So it's genuine.'

'I think Frank had no idea that the piece of papyrus fragment would lead to such a spectacular discovery. He used it because he thought it was worthless but might gain more financial support from that Smith guy.'

'Well, in the end, it's going to preserve Frank's legacy. A whole history of the Oracle of Amun. Including its prophecies. And what looks like a complete list of all the pharaohs of Egypt.'

Michael surveyed the refurbished Registry building with grim satisfaction and then looked at Anna and smiled.

Printed in Great Britain
by Amazon

45063515R00156